# BEAUTIFUL DELUSIONS
## A Dark Why Choose University Romance

## Maddison Cole

Dirty Talk Publishing Ltd

# COPYRIGHT

*Beautiful Delusions*

Maddison Cole

First published in Great Britain in [2024] by DIRTY TALK PUBLISHING LIMITED

Copyright © [2024] by [Maddison Cole]

The moral right of [Pen Name] to be identified as the author of this work has been asserted by her in accordance with the Copyright, Designs and Patents Act 1988.

All the characters in this book are fictitious, and any resemblance to actual persons living or dead, is purely coincidental.

All rights reserved. No part of this publication may be reproduced in any form or by any electronic or mechanical means, including information storage and retrieval systems, or transmitted in any form or by any means without the prior permission in writing of the copyright owner, except for the use of quotation in book reviews.

To request permission, contact authormaddisoncole@gmail.com

ASBN: B0BQFSYMM5

Edited by: J. Preston

Cover Design: Dialerie Graphic Arts

Published by DIRTY TALK PUBLISHING LTD

For everyone who dreams to survive.

For every bookworm who reads to escape.

## Trigger Warnings:

This is a Why Choose romance, meaning the female lead will have three love interests and refuse to pick only one. Dark themes such as schizophrenia, hallucinations, medication, depression and such are included. Expect excessive amounts of steam, violence and cursing throughout.

Tropes include enemies-to-lovers, high school bullies, forced proximity, power plays and multiple partner sex scenes.

## Please Note:

Mental health is no laughing matter, and this author is acutely aware of the struggles so many of us face. This book is a piece of fiction, intended to entertain. Rest assured, in no way, shape or form, is Maddison suggesting anyone should stop taking their medication in the hopes three billionaire step brothers appear to drown you in dick. Please seek the advise of a medical professional before making any changes to your prescription.

Without further ado, please enjoy Sophia's story – which is 100% NOT a self-help guide.

# CONTENTS

1. Chapter One — 1
2. Chapter Two — 11
3. Chapter Three — 17
4. Chapter Four — 25
5. Chapter Five — 30
6. Chapter Six — 33
7. Chapter Seven — 42
8. Chapter Eight — 49
9. Chapter Nine — 57
10. Chapter Ten — 64
11. Chapter Eleven — 72
12. Chapter Twelve — 76
13. Chapter Thirteen — 80
14. Chapter Fourteen — 85
15. Chapter Fifteen — 92
16. Chapter Sixteen — 100
17. Chapter Seventeen — 110
18. Chapter Eighteen — 115

| 19. | Chapter Nineteen | 122 |
| 20. | Chapter Twenty | 135 |
| 21. | Chapter Twenty One | 143 |
| 22. | Chapter Twenty Two | 150 |
| 23. | Chapter Twenty Three | 155 |
| 24. | Chapter Twenty Four | 165 |
| 25. | Chapter Twenty Five | 173 |
| 26. | Epilogue | 180 |
| 27. | Acknowledgements | 185 |
| 28. | About the Author | 187 |
| 29. | Other Works | 189 |

## Chapter 1

Do you believe in déjà vu? How about the pre-emptive feeling something bad is about to happen? That's what I've had since the moment I opened my eyes.

The fourth university. The fourth chance to get things right. Staring at the ceiling, I search inside myself, trying to find the will to move. All it would take is one easy slide for my leg to slip out from beneath the covers, and my foot to hit the carpeted floor. But it's what comes after that has me seized in place. The darkness will seep in, plaguing me with whispers of failure. My fingers twitch for the nearest book I could lose myself in, but if I don't show up on the first day, I'll find myself thrown out once again.

Struck with an impending panic attack, I just lie there, ramrod straight on my back.

*"You know, there are a decent amount of ways you could make a living whilst lying on your back."* A voice cuts through my thoughts. Not a real voice within the room, but one that emanates from inside my head. *"At least then you won't have to make an ass of yourself at this new fancy school. Not like the last one."* I shudder, batting my hand in her general direction. The figure in my peripheral quickly dissipates. There are certain instances where she appears, taunting me with fantastical ideas which usually end me up in more trouble.

*"Besides, you never really wanted a master's degree anyway,"* the voice slips through my groaning once more. I roll my head aside. Her dark-haired mirage is leaning against my new dorm dresser, chewing on a wad of bubblegum and raising her eyebrow. Jazzie, in all her cocky, tattooed glory, looks at me knowingly with hazel eyes. *"This was your get-out-of-jail-free card. No one would blame you if you quit and spent the rest of your life with your legs in the air and covered in cum."* Okay, fine, I'm getting up.

Stumbling directly through her image, I search in the dark for the bathroom light. It was late when I arrived last night, my roommate had already fallen asleep as I paced around outside with my headphones on, delaying the inevitable. This is my last chance to complete my master's; the last school which would accept my colorful record.

Locating the light and my make-up bag, I scramble for my pill bottles. *Klonopin* for anxiety, *Clozapine* for the rest. Any will do. Anything to calm the nerves, the voices. To clear my brain of the hallucinations which will plague me otherwise. It never used to be like this. Once upon a time, I had friends who weren't imaginary. Now I talk to myself for comfort.

Closing my hand around the first bottle, I give an instinctual shake. *Empty.* The next one, *empty.* Upending the bag into the basin, my brows furrow, a sinking feeling in the pit of my chest growing. Every single bottle is light and hollow. *No.* That can't be right; I had fresh refills only the day before yesterday.

"*I wonder how much your antipsychotics would fetch on the black market,*" that same feminine voice chuckles. I spin with a scowl. Highlights of silver in Jazzie's ruffled hair shimmer in the LEDs, black leather cinching her body in all the right places. The black ink spilling across her saturated skin seamlessly blends from one skull into the next, amidst a sea of shaded roses. I continue to stare, expecting her to flitter away from existence. Instead, she chews and pops her gum, the sound loud enough in my ears to make me flinch.

"Wait, what did you say?" My mind relays her words like a phone line with a bad connection. The. Black. Market. My gut plummets. My feet scrape across the tile as I drive through Jazzie this time, ripping my roommate's covers from the adjacent bed. Striking my fist onto the shadowed, lumpy outline, memory foam cushions my knuckles. I hit again and again, a shriek escaping me. I haven't even met the fucker I'm supposed to spend the rest of the semester with, and they've already *stolen* from me. My lungs squeeze, holding my last breath hostage.

I had it planned perfectly. I've spent weeks daydreaming about every inevitable situation, replaying it over and over. Pouring over the campus maps, working out the routes to best avoid large crowds. I've imagined what it'll be like to share a room again, and all the ways I can distract myself from their lingering presence.

"It's fine," I wheeze, attempting to reassure someone. I'm not exactly sure who. Collapsing on the bed, my legs automatically curl into a fetal position. "It's totally fine. I only need to attend the registration meeting this morning. Everything else was voluntary. It's just a couple of hours, and then I can grab some more meds before classes start tomorrow. It's just a couple of hours," I clench the covers in my fist, rocking gently. My biceps tremble until my diaphragm finally burns enough to release the air in a gust of relief. "Just a couple of hours."

"*You know as well as I do,*" Jazzie murmurs, "*the pharmacist won't replace your prescription so soon. Even if you didn't have to rely on the insurance, you're utterly fucked. And not in the good sense.*" I tune her out. Endless rage simmers so close to the surface, I could hurl this bed out of the closest window, myself joining right behind. The mental image is enough of a dampener to relax my shoulders.

This was supposed to be my fresh start. No one knows me here; no one needs to know the schizophrenic wreck I truly am. And with that thought in mind, I numbly force myself to wash, dress, shoulder my backpack, and storm out of the room.

Hordes of people line the hallway, a few stares catching my eye as I push my way through the middle, not bothering to strike up any conversations. As always, my blue hair falls forward to shield my face. A thick, straight curtain I hide behind, in the same pale aquamarine as my eyes. Stained carpets lead the way to a concrete stairwell, littered with so many discarded blobs of gum even Jazzie scoffs beside my ear.

"*What a waste*," she mutters. I'm too busy trying to avoid each one like a rubbery maze waiting to ensnare my white Converse. If that wasn't bad enough, I'd hazard a guess the cleaners don't attend to the worn, once-cream railing and stained walls which smell too much like vomit and urine to be anything else. Seems I opted for the front, cleaner entrance when I arrived last night, or I never would have made it up to my room.

With a small stroke of luck, I don't think will continue, I make it to the ground floor and out the rear fire escape without a single mark on my sneakers or short denim skirt. I tug on the left sleeve of my oversized lilac sweater, a nervous habit I've developed to hide what's underneath. The sweater doesn't match the rest of my outfit, but I wasn't focused on fashion. Merely surviving Jazzie's judgmental stare.

The dorm block is a beast of brick and one of twelve, divided into male and female residences depending on which side of the main road you are on. I'd originally entered by foot on the far south side of campus, abandoned by bus and forced to trek through streams of frat houses and sororities. Or as I prefer to call them, '*Entitled Living for the Rich and Ridiculous*'. Now the morning sun dances across the campus, a central clock tower is visible in the distance. I follow a tarmac road towards the main buildings, keeping to the grassy bank, which provides no sidewalk. Headphones on, background drowned out.

I'm mentally visualizing the map in my mind's eyes when sports cars whizz by, containing a bunch of assholes shouting something incoherent from open-top roofs. I turn my face away, letting them pass by without the response they're seeking. Approaching the barriers of a huge parking lot, I duck right and take a detour. The trail is muddy and manmade, tracking a ten-foot fence to the lecture halls. Once I reach the end, I speed through carefully cultivated gardens, keeping my back to an outbuilding which contains the gym and swimming pool. Even from here, chlorine clogs the air and the gym-heads jog on by.

Setting my jaw, I tackle the maze of halls, taking a huge detour before I exit opposite where I'm going to hide most of the time—the main library. I almost cave, lulled in my the false pretense of no one being nearby. Climbing the stone stairs, I see Jazzie waiting by the entrance, knowing smirk on her face. My nostrils flare. I can't let them win. So instead, I remove my headphones and stride for the student center next door. Seniors smile from the front desk, surrounded by more leaflets than workspace.

"Can I help you?" the girl asks before her male companion gets the chance. Both look too clean, too well put together for this time in the morning. All brunette hair, beaming smiles, and smart shirts holding name tags. Jazzie's voice flitters through my mind, advising me to ask where the nurse's office is. Nurses have drugs. We like drugs.

"No," I shake my head, wrinkling up my nose. Kyra, as her nametag states, raises her brows. "I mean yes, please. I'm looking for Dean O'Sullivan's office. I have a registration meeting at…" I trail off, catching sight of the large clock beyond the reception area. One. Hour. Ago. "Dammit it," I curse under my breath.

"I'm afraid the Dean had to attend to a situation and has back-to-back meetings for the rest of the day. I presume you're Sophia Chambers? This was left for you," she removes a large brown envelope from a drawer behind the desk. It's heavy, as I imagine the weight of my previous transcripts would be.

I peer inside just as Kyra begins to reel off everything I should have. Program module, timetable, equipment requirements, a reading list I'm expected to have completed, an invite to join the student government, and due to my situation–as she so kindly put it–a preloaded card for restaurants and cafes on site. As part of the agreement I signed electronically before being accepted here, I was told of the monthly allowance I would have access to under the terms of my specialist scholarship. Something I hope Kyra and no one else knows of. Gripping the envelope tightly, a wash of relief hits me as I turn towards the automatic doors. It's done, I'm free for the rest of the day.

"Miss Chambers?" a voice stops me as I'm about to leave. I turn my head, startled by the clicking of heels growing closer.

"Um…yes?" I swallow hard. The woman keeps advancing, directly into my personal space. Holding out a poised palm, her smile is as tight as the bun pulling back her dark hair. I hesitantly shake her hand.

"I'm so glad I caught you. Lorna Mitchell, Assistant Dean. Call me Lorna, everyone does. Can I have a word?" Jerking her head towards the hallways she's approached from, my eyes widen. I've had video calls with Dean O'Sullivan; I've read his online bio. I don't know Lorna Mitchell.

"It won't take long," Lorna senses my hesitation. Kyra is watching intently from the desk, clearly expecting me to make a run for it. Ducking my head, I follow Lorna to an office without a window. No escape, I realize as the door is closed behind me. "Relax Sophia, I don't bite." Ignoring Lorna's small laugh, my eyes trail over her office.

"I don't handle surprises well," I mutter to myself. Polished mahogany furniture, shelves lined with leather-bound books, university memorabilia in a glass cabinet. Framed degrees hang on the sickly floral wallpaper, surrounding a doctorate in the center.

"I specialize in psychology," Lorna announces proudly, although I find myself under her watchful gaze. Fantastic. Gripping the envelope to my chest, I sit in the intended chair, using it as a barrier between the Assistant Dean and my beating heart. Jazzie settles cross-legged on the floor, stroking what appears to be an evil kitty.

"Now then," Lorna smiles tightly again. I vaguely wonder if it's the harshness of her hairstyle or the tight bodice of her pantsuit restricting her from showing true emotion. "I felt it important for us to get to know one another and set up regular weekly meetings so you have a safe place to talk. Adjustments can be tricky, but you can always request to see me when needed." I don't respond, a lump forming in my throat. I know better than anyone how 'tricky' adjustments can be. That's why I do everything in my power to pre-empt them.

"It's healthy to know someone is on hand, even if it's just to touch base. We have a wealth of counselors and student groups dedicated to mental health, but I thought you might prefer something a little more...intimate."

"You know of my history." My cheeks flare. I shouldn't be embarrassed, and it was foolish to think my details were only shared with the Dean himself. Lorna doesn't shrink away from the conversation like I do.

"I'm on the board of directors. We all discussed your request to be placed in a dormitory on your own." My brows immediately furrow, my tongue let loose before I can catch it.

"So it's your fault," I snap out of nowhere. Lorna doesn't flinch, but I do. "Sorry. I just–it's just easier when I'm on my own. It would have caused me a lot less stress if I had a place of solace."

"I do understand, especially given your past," Lorna appears sympathetic. It quickly vanishes. "However, the last university you attended had to pry you out of your room. You missed classes on a daily basis and barricaded yourself in with a wall of books. Socializing may not come easily to you, but it could help to have some encouragement. Your roommate has been carefully chosen to ensure you're encouraged to go to class and study." I scoff. Yeah, my roommate is a thieving fucking saint. An emotion crosses Lorna's face, which is too close to pity for my liking. "We all want what's best for you, Sophia."

"Understood," I nod woodenly. "Weekly meetings and a roommate to force me out of my room. Is that everything?" Jazzie looks up at my face, booming with pride. I'm not being rude intentionally, but once the mask of fear slips, there's nothing underneath to cushion my mood. I'm a shell of regret and irritation unless my head is in a book. Lorna doesn't stop my exit, telling me to make our appointment at the reception as the door slips closed between us. I do just that, with the alternative being that Lorna will track me down with surprise meetings I can't prepare for.

Nodding my thanks to Kyra, I leave on numb legs, pausing outside the electronic doors. Classes don't start until tomorrow, but I wish I had the distraction now. Looking towards the library, I feel the tug. The pull of a thousand worlds ready to be unleashed on my mind, to fill my dreams with words where acceptance comes so easily. Where love truly exists. I'm halfway there without realizing it when my shoe skids to a stop, a small voice reaching my ears.

"Billions of ice and rock fragments. Billions of ice and dust. No, wait...was it..." Peering around the corner, an alcove against the student block becomes visible. Wooden in structure, a pointed roof shrouded in layers of wisteria, white as jasmine and swaying gently over the entrance. Through the gaps, I see her sitting on a bench only big enough to seat two. A timid girl with bunched shoulders. Thin, pale, and wringing the strap of a handbag in her lap, chewing on her marred bottom lip. "Yes, that's it. The fragments are torn apart by Saturn's gravity. Billions of ice and rock fragments coated in dust form the rings. I think. Oh fuck, wait no–"

I step closer, intent on asking if she's okay when I hear that tell-tale sound. The shake of a plastic bottle, the pop of a cap. I still, my heart kicking up a beat. Using her bag as a shield, she can't hide the small blue pill in her open palm from me.

"Is that Valium?!" I'm unable to hold myself back, bursting through the flowers to invade her sanctuary. She yelps, flinching as if she can also see Jazzie in my peripheral, swirling a baseball bat around. Plastering a look of concern on my face, I lower beside her knees. A stranger filled with compassion, only looking out for her wellbeing.

*"Yeah, right,"* Jazzie chuckles in my head. A series of unnerving instructions follow to get that pill at any cost.

"It...it's my last one, and I need to relax if I'm going to be able to study. Professor Harrison always starts the semester with a quiz." The girl is shaking, riddled with an anxiety I know all too well. The blonde in her hair has grown out, brown roots tracing her scalp to where it's tucked behind her ears. Her eyes are wide, glazed as if she might just burst into tears, and her entire being would turn into a puddle at my feet.

"I hear you. Tests can be stressful, but believe me," I shift to sit by her side, eyeing the pill in her open palm, "you're strong. You've already studied, right?" She nods. "Then you must believe in yourself, face your fears, and prove you're worth more than your nerves allow."

Relaying back what multiple therapists have told me, my responding smile is watery, hiding my desperation. This is for her own good. Maybe a little encouragement is all she needs. Fuck knows, all I need is right there, inches away, with a V printed on the pill.

"Here, let me dispose of that for you. No one needs to know." I slowly raise my fingers. She sits a little straighter, tracking my movements like a rabbit about to bolt. I'm cautious, not once rushing. Not when my own hand begins to shake, an eager sweat breaking out across my brow. My pinkie grazes her wrist, jolting her into action. Her palm moves within a blink, that precious blue pill thrust into her mouth and swallowed on a whimper. I gape at her.

*"She's going to run for it,"* Jazzie warns as the girl clings to her bag and does just that. Although, she's not fast enough. Fisting her hair, my actions aren't my own as she shrieks, and I hastily cover her mouth.

"You must know where to get more. Tell me," I ground out, intent on dragging her body a step back into the shadows of the building. Adrenaline burns through my muscles with the effort to hold her in place, while Jazzie's voice in my head coaxes me onward. *'Wring the answers from her. Show her who you really are.'* I shudder, realizing what I'm doing. This isn't who I really am, or at least not who I want to be. Preparing to release the poor girl, muttering sounds through my hand.

"There's a party," she rasps as I give her an inch to speak. "Tonight, Thorn Manor. Ask for Lucas. He…he can get you whatever you want." Her large eyes are full of tears as she looks up at me, the fear I'm pouring into her working against her Valium. Releasing her, I duck back into the alcove, hiding long after she's fled. Raking my hands through my blue hair,

I pace around Jazzie, ignoring the approval she tries to give. She can't keep making me do that. I'm not supposed to be that person anymore.

Clinging to the hope the girl won't squeal to the nearest person who will listen, I calm my erratic breathing. In for three, out for five, until my chest unclenches. Lucas can get whatever I want. That's the new focus. I have a whole day until this party, until any hopes of getting some form of release. Snatching up my brown envelope from the ground, I root around inside for my café card and hold it like a lifeline. If I don't have drugs, I'll take the next best thing. Coffee.

## Chapter 2

"What do you mean, my card isn't *valid*?! I just got it," I seethe over the counter. My knuckles are white, and nostrils are fully flared. Some preppy douchebag, with his polo shirt buttoned to the top, holds up a finger, placing a quick call before coming back to me.

"The cards are valid from the first day of full enrolment," he looks me up and down like I have fleas, "which for you is tomorrow." The scent of caffeine, the clang of machinery, the hiss of steam all mock me as I hold up the line. Bunching my shoulders, I scowl, silently wishing a violent case of diarrhea on this asshole before stalking away. No drugs, no fucking coffee. What's next? Slamming my hands into the glass door, my sneakers hit the ground harder than necessary. There's only one place left to go.

Once more, Jazzie is waiting at the top of the library steps. I should have given up and come here in the first instance. Poised within a pointed archway, framed by intricate stone carvings, I need to use my weight against the wooden door for it to creak open. This building, like the clock tower across the courtyard, must be one of the last remaining from the original campus. Slipping inside, several floors of railings meet my gaze.

Connected by winding staircases, I find myself in the center, levels bellowing out into the ground below as well as towering above. Grand chandeliers glimmer against brass railings, the tarnished color at odds with the wrinkled and cracked spines of first editions. Dust circulates the scent of aged paper. The breath is knocked from me long before someone shoves open the door, slamming into my back. Growling, I shuffle forward.

My mind is distracted as I approach the main desk, scribbling out my details on a registration form. The bookcases, the shelves. So many shelves. So many spines waiting for their stories to be revealed. This is where I feel safe. Where worlds of heartbreak and angst await. This is where I feel sane.

"Sophia," a harsh voice snaps. I whip my head back to the woman behind the desk, her plaque naming her as Head Librarian - Mrs. Russell.

"Um, did you say something?" I blink rapidly. The gray-haired woman is well past retirement age, her back hunched from the weight of carrying heavy paperbacks for the past forty-odd years. The kind who will work here until she's forced out by new management, and then probably volunteer to dust the banisters until she dies. I grow dazed, realizing I can see myself becoming the next Mrs. Russell. Her bones creak like the bookshelves as she snatches the pen from my hand.

"I'm locking up at ten sharp, whether you're in or out. If you spill tea on a book, you pay for its replacement," her gnarled finger points to a table across the platform. It's simple, foldable on metal legs with a cloth draped over the plastic top. A singular hot water tank steams beside a random assortment of mugs, mostly chipped, an open box of tea bags, a jug of milk, and a heap of sweetener packets fulfilling the complimentary refreshments. Not coffee, but I'll take whatever I can get at this point.

## CHAPTER TWO

Accepting my new library card, I fix a tea and lose myself amongst the shelves. Two levels down, I find what I'm looking for. Dark romance, typically in a seedy, shadowed section with a beanbag in the corner. I don't dare touch it, not without my UV light to inspect it first. Lifting out a random book, the first one I spot with 'wrath' in the title, I settle cross-legged on the floor where Jazzie is already waiting. Prying open the front cover, I release a heavy sigh, emptying my mind as I dive in.

\*\*\*

The lights go out. I jolt, splashing cold tea over the rim of the mug, pattering the denim of my skirt. As long as it didn't stain the pages–that's all I care about. It takes a moment of reeling to realize I'm on the last few chapters of the book in my hand, time lost to me as much as my hold on reality. It's not uncommon for me to check out completely. Not when fiction is where my heart thrives.

Blinking through purple-rimmed glasses, I don't remember pulling out of my bag, I squint at the overhead lights. The bulbs glow faintly as they cool, fading into darkness. A few levels above, light seeps from elongated windows, spiraling the railing like a ring of everlasting sunset. The breeze drifts downward, cutting through the balmy air with a blissful caress. No wonder it was so easy to lose myself in a world so distant from this one.

Placing down the mug, I uncurl my legs from beneath me on the floor. Laying the book down, pages splayed over my thighs, I stretch in half, holding my toes to work some feeling back into my legs. Then I draw them back into a cross-seated position, and I roll my neck. Jazzie mirrors my every movement, leaning against the opposite shelves, one brow cocked. I know what she's thinking–obviously–I've heard it before. A uni grad student like myself should be outside, *living my life*. Well, life generally sucks, and I'm happy exactly where I am. As long as it's quiet and I'm medicated....*shit*. The time. The party.

Jumping upright, panic floods my system. My movements are jaunted as I drag myself up the shelves, pausing to slip the book back in its rightful place. Then I'm down the aisle as fast as my feet will allow. I've missed it. I've fucked it. My chance to get more meds.

Today was difficult enough, and getting through tomorrow will be impossible. The weight of oppression crashes down on my shoulders, a blaring of a siren sounding between my ears. Pins and needles race from my toes to calves, forcing me to hobble. The skirt grazes my thighs, in direct contrast with the baggy lilac sweatshirt covering me from neck to wrists. Too hot. Too itchy against my taunt skin. I've fucking fucked it all.

*Slam.*

A hard body sends me flying backward. I hit the ground, pain slicing along my back as my assailant stands firm. Unaffected. The fading sunlight frames his broad shoulders, his jersey too baggy to reveal what's underneath. But I felt it. The solid muscle, the radiating power. I wait for him to move or speak, to offer me a hand. A mess of light hair shifts so slightly. His head tilt could merely be a trick of the shadows, but somehow I don't think so.

"Who are you?" His voice is like melted butter, too smooth. I vaguely wonder if he's real, or a figment of my vivid imagination. But I feel the drag of his gaze on my bare legs, which have remained at an awkward angle and giving his heated stare full access.

"*There're two ways this is going to play out,*" Jazzie shuffles closer on her knees. She appears bright amongst the shelves, as if she has her own light source, and drapes an arm over my shoulders. "*You can fight him or fuck him. Either one will give you the release your precious drugs would have otherwise provided.*" I balk, blinking hard in the hopes she'll disappear. My attacker is yet to move while my mind plays out the scenario, "*You've missed the party anyway. Might as well use the goods at your disposal.*" Jazzie leans forward and grabs his junk roughly. My eyes widen until he clears his throat as I realize I was staring straight at his dick.

Clambering to my feet, I brush myself down. Two sets of eyes are on me, one real and one imaginary. I can hardly breathe, the burden in my chest overbearing. If I walk away now, head back to my dorm, I'll lie awake all night. Replaying how I wished this encounter had gone. I'm new here, no one knows me. He doesn't know my past. He'll only see the person I present now, and first impressions are everything.

"I could be whoever you want me to be," I pull a smile from the depths of my psyche. Jazzie smiles approvingly, slinking out of sight. This close up, the faintest scent of apple and an underlying musk drifts through me, like cider on a summer's night.

"Excuse me?" he scoffs, folding his arms. Biceps bulge over a basketball jersey, his stance wide against the slip of light I have left. He's athletic, strong. Probably able to bench press me and keep the cocky tilt of his head while he does it. A fuckboy, no doubt, and luckily that's what I'm in the market for. A quick release to get me through until my next fix. Closing the gap between us, I force myself to embody the female character who lives rent free in my head.

"We're alone, in the dark, and I'm bored." I summon confidence from deep within, trailing my fingers over his shoulder where the jersey cuts short, his skin smooth and blemish free. He might as well be a delusion. Uncrossing his arms, the sheer size of him has my heart thumping loud enough for us both to hear it. He absorbs the very air around us. Even without seeing him properly, the way he holds himself tells me what I need to know. He's freaking gorgeous and knows it.

"I'm not into nerds," he slides my glasses off and places them on a nearby shelf. "I only came in here to restock my paper stash." Diving a hand into his pocket, he produces a wad of rolled pages, all torn roughly. A fissure cracks through my heart, but I don't let it show. He smokes, most likely weed, meaning he's a friend I need to keep close. This stubborn ball-player might just be able to see me through my final semester. Then I'm a free woman.

"I'm not into asshole jocks, but somehow, I think we both can pretend otherwise for a little while." Brazenly, my fingers continue to travel over his biceps, along his arms. Moving with the swiftness of a cheetah, my wrists are grabbed, and I'm shoved back a step against the bookcase.

"You proposition me and then have the balls to call me an asshole?" he growls. I smile encouragingly.

"I'm Sophia," I bat my lashes. His grip on my wrists tightens. Yes, I think to myself. This is the distraction I need. The release I crave. Dropping his head, close enough for his breath to tangle with mine, for his strong jaw to brush my cheek, he pauses. Sizing me up, studying the heavy rise and fall of my chest. If only he could see my nipples through this heavy sweater, he'd understand how ready I am to be ruined. Corrupted. Defiled.

"Now you give me your name," I coax.

"Nah. You're definitely not my type." Using his grip to shove himself back and stride away, red coats my vision. Shame heats my cheeks. Holy crap. What the fuck was I thinking–throwing myself at a stranger in the dark? Nothing, that's what. I wasn't thinking at all. And it's that same empty numbness pulsing through my veins which has my Converse appearing in my hand and tumbling away from me in a full-bodied throw. The sneaker hits him in the back of the head.

"The fuck–" his growl is cut short by a round of laughter. Shadows appear at his back. This time, I'm certain they're not from my imagination.

"I believe your new friend wants your attention, Ezra," another male voice seeps from the darkness. I can't see them, can't tell how many there are, but a symphony of low chuckles grows in volume, gritty and rough like dirt being kicked up from the ground. Whatever parallel universe I'd been in, where fear and lust mingled, vanishes. My true senses return in their entirety.

"She can have my attention if she likes," another voice sounds. Filled with mirth, not half as deep and rumbling as the last. A ball forms in my throat.

"You know what? I have somewhere else to be. So, I'm just gonna…" my voice trails off as I fail to find a way to say '*run for my fucking life*'. Instead, I just do it.

## Chapter 3

I'd already left the main courtyard before remembering my backpack. Forgotten on the library floor, I make a mental note to head back first thing in the morning to retrieve it. For now, though, I'm left without my phone, dorm keys, and my legs covered in scratches from the library window I'd managed to dive out of. I barely feel them through the tremors of withdrawal and embarrassment causing me to stomp too heavily. But I refuse to stop running.

In my haste, I lose sight of the trail I was supposed to take, thundering forward in the hopes those stoners find someone better to play with. I still can't believe what I allowed myself to do, and now all my hopes are pinned on my roommate still being awake. Only, when I emerge from the other path I sped down, I can't see the dorm buildings.

I draw to a quick stop before two rows of frat houses instead. All are quiet and dark, except the whitewashed walled structure halfway down the street. That one is glowing from the inside out, while music pulsates through the air. Laughter and chatter mingle with the bass. Nearing on numb feet, I swallow hard. Letters carved over the doorway fill me with a surge of trepidation.

*Thorn Manor.* It's not too late. The party is still going in full swing.

People spill out onto the front lawn. The energy is infectious, despite my hesitation of being around so many other people. My instincts are telling me to seek out the reprieve of my dorm building, but leaving now wouldn't help my cause. I need something; a temporary high to get me through the next day or so. I won't survive otherwise.

Besides, no one is looking at me. Words are slurring, and visions appear hazy. I'm a nobody amongst the masses, and with the gentle press of Jazzie in the back of my mind, I suddenly find myself at the front door. Drawn in like a moth to a flame, liveliness reverberates through my body.

Inside, the air is thick with the scent of alcohol and sweat. Bodies move in synchronized chaos, passing around drinks. People are making out on any available surface. One group is containing a small fire on the coffee table in a lavish living area and cheering as each one drops another item into the center of it.

Jazzie leads me onward, further through the crowds and into the heart of Thorn Manor. The music grows louder as we descend a flight of stairs, leading us to a basement filled with even more dancers. The room is transformed into a makeshift nightclub, bodies pressed together, moving to the pounding beat. Neon lights flash across the dimly lit room, casting vibrant hues on the unknown faces. My temples clench tightly.

"Nope, no thanks." I back out. Regardless of what's brought me to be here, that's too many people in too small a space. Staggering back into the lobby, my stomach rolls. For the second time tonight, I can't believe I've allowed myself to enter a viper's nest. Desperation to rid myself of this anxious itch is pushing me into even more triggering situations, and so the spiral continues.

"*You have to play the part,*" Jazzie chastises me, appearing at my side. Her leather dress is tight-fitting and dips far too low into her sternum. I look down at my own outfit–a baggy sweater, short skirt and one muddy foot which will definitely need some medical attention later. "*You can't waltz into a party and start demanding for a drug dealer. Smile, flutter your lashes. It'll get you further, trust me.*" I twist behind a huge central staircase, stealing a moment to myself. She's right, I need to be discrete but appealing.

Straightening my sweater, kicking off my other sneaker, and flicking my straight, blue hair over my shoulder, I re-emerge to throw flirty smiles and winks out like hooks amongst the fishes. Never mind that I'm still panting from my midnight sprint, or reeling over the need to curl up in a ball and cry. Confidence is key, and that's what begins drawing a pack of hot guys towards me. I don't let them get too close, slipping through a set of French sliding doors to the back patio before I start to hyperventilate.

It's much less crowded and easier to breathe out here, the rounded patio a much-needed solid base beneath my feet. Beside an oval swimming pool, a table is covered in a black cloth and all kinds of spirits and drinks. I'm not supposed to drink on my meds, but I'm also not going to survive this night sober. A bartender in a slick shirt rolled up to the elbows is spinning glasses and bottles around him in an impressive display, drawing us closer.

"What can I get you?" he asks, handing a bright pink cocktail to another guest, complete with cherry and umbrella.

"One of those would do the trick." I nod assertively. I watch the bartender repeat his juggling act, his eyes flicking to me curiously every few seconds. I know what he's thinking; I've heard it before. 'Why's a pretty girl like you by herself?' People assume my fuller lips and pale blue eyes, my long legs, and lithe shape should be enough to gain me popularity. But I can't keep long-term friends from the habit of shutting everyone out. Accepting my drink, I sip it gingerly. I haven't eaten much today to justify knocking it back and grabbing for another.

Suddenly, arms grip me from behind, dragging me sideways. A scream is torn from my throat as air whooshes past my ears, the glass flying from my hand. Colliding with the pool, the iron grip clinging onto my mid-section doesn't loosen, holding me beneath the water. Bubbles escape my mouth as I cry out, writhing in the banded arms. As my lungs begin to ache, a slice of dread takes over, forcing my elbow to connect with a strong jaw. Releasing me at last, I frantically kick upwards, making sure to hit my attacker once more along the way.

Breaching the surface, laughter rings out all around the pool's edge. I swim to a metal ladder, pulling my weight up whilst ignoring the multiple smartphones being shoved in my face. The crowd automatically departs, allowing my gaze to settle on a guy reclining in a sun lounger with sunglasses on, despite the moon being directly overhead. What a douche.

"I'm glad you seem amused," I seethe when he does nothing but smirk at me. I tug on my left sleeve, awkward beneath the weight of his, and everyone else's, attention.

"That's what happens to uninvited guests, I'm afraid," he says before downing the contents of his whiskey glass. A golden chain hangs over his white t-shirt beneath an open leather jacket, dark jeans hugging his legs above a pair of unlaced timberlands. Girls are fawning over him, massaging different areas of his body.

A figure bursting upwards from the water makes me flinch, an unnecessary amount of water being splashed over my legs. His legs move back and forth, keeping him afloat as I notice the basketball jersey floating around his muscled arms. A mop of dark blond hair is plastered to his head, his eyes boring into mine with more than a little hatred. It's him, from the library. *Ezra*.

Of all the stupid reasons, for the love of unbroken opinions, my first thought upon seeing him is...he didn't bring my damn shoe. He's halfway up the ladder when a white flash of rage comes over me, striking my heel into his chest. He slips, caught off guard and splashes back beneath the surface. Some people cheer, most gasp, and that's when I know, I've really fucked up. A hand slips through the crowd, grabbing my wrist and dragging me away. I sense the douche watching me leave from beneath his sunglasses, although he makes no move to stop me. Why would he?

The hand doesn't stop tugging until we're back in the manor, rounding the stairs. A head of strawberry blonde hair bobs ahead, a sickly-sweet voice muttering to herself. Reaching a bedroom, she orders the threesome currently taking place on the ottoman to get lost. Strangely enough, they obey, leaving just the two of us alone.

"I don't know what you did to piss Ezra off, but a word to the wise, don't do it again," she raises a single brow at me before breaking into a huge smile. "I'm Letty." Her hand slips into mine, giving it an involuntary shake.

"Um, hi. I'm Sophia," I lower my head as if I'm ashamed of my own name. Somehow, despite the crowds which were just surrounding me, it's Letty's closeness which unnerves me the most. Her energy is expansive, drawing any I had left directly from my soul.

"Come on, let's get you cleaned up. You look like shit," she giggles. Leaving me against the closed door, Letty rummages through some drawers, then a wardrobe and lastly, looks under the bed. "Here you go," she deposits a heap of material into my arms, topped with glittering chunky heels.

After being directed to a bathroom, any debate I had dies on my tongue as I see the mirror. Damn, I do look like shit. My makeup is smudged, my hair is a tangled mess, and there are bruises forming on my arms from the struggle in the pool. My eyes drop to the glittery dress I've been supplied, already knowing I can't wear that. It's too…exposed. But that's a future me problem.

Stripping out of my wet clothes, I shiver as the cold air hits my skin before stepping into the shower. I should be in more of a rush, but once the heated water touches my skin, I lose all sense of place and time. Letting the warmth wash away the chlorine, I wait out the fear still lingering in my psyche. Outside this spray, there are hordes of students waiting. Watching for what I might do next. There's an asshole who called me out for being a stranger and another who threw me into the pool. My legs shake, threatening to give out. I'm trapped. In the middle of a nightmare with no way to escape.

*Breathe, Sophia.* Jazzie sounds in my mind. She doesn't appear in the bathroom or when I'm at my most vulnerable, but she's still there in the back of my head. *Stop thinking and breathe.*

"I c-c-can't. I can't, I-I can't," my voice tremors. My chest spasms, causing the rest of my limbs to shake. I know these signs. I need to reel myself in because there's no stopping the avalanche once it tips over the edge of the mountain. In the midst of my labored breathing, the bathroom walls start to close in on me. The once soothing water now feels suffocating, as if it's trying to drown me instead of washing away my fears. I claw at the tiled walls, desperately trying to find an anchor, something to ground me and pull me back from the abyss. But the panic engulfs me, swallowing me whole. My vision blurs and the sound of rushing water transforms into a deafening roar. I'm drowning, not in a pool of chlorine, but in the sea of my own turmoil.

"The fuck?" a voice cuts through the void. I vaguely realize the shower door is opening, but there's no time or strength to cover myself. The water abruptly halts. Strong arms gather me up from the crumbled position on the floor I didn't realize I was in. My skin is raw and tender from where I've unknowingly scrubbed myself too hard, unable to shake off the image of Ezra's furious eyes. He's not going to forgive any of my actions from tonight, and as far as social suicide goes, I reckon I've just signed my own death warrant.

"You're safe," a deep voice grumbles, the vibration rolling beneath my cheek. I think he meant to be kind, but aided by a fierce kick to slam the door closed, the valiant rescue comes off as a huge inconvenience. I cower, naked and vulnerable, against his chest. The vulnerability is overwhelming, but there's also a strange sense of comfort in his embrace. His touch is gentle as if he understands the fragile state of my being. Keeping the lights dimmed and wrapping me in a fluffy towel, he places me on the bed. I resist looking up at his towering outline. My panic attack subsides straight back into a state of fear. I've been in some awkward situations in my life; naked and wet on a bed with a stranger isn't one of them.

*Whatever the fuck you do,* Jazzie comments in my ears, *do not proposition him.* I could scowl at her. She's the reason I'm in this mess.

"You must think I'm really stupid." I take a shaky breath, steadying myself as I meet his gaze. His eyes, too dark to discern a color, hold a glimmer of something too akin to understanding. I shrink into myself. It's as if he can see through my carefully constructed facade, stripping me bare of the layers of deflection I've spent years putting in place. I'm the pretty girl that hides in books; that's my personality. But the way he's lingering over me now, I wish I seemed like more. That I was more.

"Not stupid. Disorientated," he finally speaks. I wish I could say the rumbling sound cutting through the air didn't make me flinch. Today is a bad day for me, and the entire school has witnessed the extent of my weakness. "I suppose this is what you came here for." Pulling a small plastic bag from his pocket, the glint of the moon highlights a singular small, rounded pill. I gasp, trying to snatch it.

"How did you—" He flicks the bag just out of my reach.

"When my lab partner missed our study session, I found her cowering in a lecture hall. Apparently, some new girl with blue hair attacked her for a Valium. The same girl with blue hair who tried to seduce Ezra in the library. I must say, if you want to be more discreet, I'd consider a different dye job."

I don't comment further as I slum back against the headboard. A part of me wants to walk out of here and never look back, but that part never shouts loud enough. My eyes track the small pill, my throat too tight to swallow. After everything I've been through today, I can't leave without it all being for a reason.

"This is my room," he raises a singular brow, "and like I said, you're safe here. I'll man the door while you do whatever it is you need to do." Tossing the small packet at me, he strides to the door with long, graceful footsteps. His jeans are fitted to perfection, his dark t-shirt a snug fit. I already knew he was muscular from the way he carried me like I weighed nothing.

"I hope you find the fix you're looking for, Sophia." He gives me a last spearing look before slipping out the door. The click between us is final, ringing out throughout the darkened room. The sound of the party is still going in full swing beyond the window; singing, laughing, and splashing. I wish I could say I didn't grab that plastic bag as soon as I'm convinced I've been left utterly alone, but I'd be lying. More than ever, I need the release. To escape the cage of my mind. To forget all the stupid shit I've done. My fingers shake as I place the pill onto my tongue and swallow without the need for water. Call it the placebo effect, but my limbs instantly melt, my chest rising fully for the first time. I manage to grab the hem of the cover, rolling myself over like a sausage roll, towel, and all.

*Well, what a turn today took,* Jazzie comments. I grunt in agreement, snuggling down for the deepest sleep I could possibly have in a stranger's bed.

## Chapter 4

"Rise and shine!" The clanging of a wooden spoon on a saucepan jerks me from a restless dream. I might as well not slept at all, the comedown from the valium hitting me like a ton of bricks. It's not that I'm an addict depending on my next hit. More like the serenity of a quiet mind is all the more noticeable when it's absent. The clanging abruptly stops, the pillow ripped away, and the morning light bursting through open curtains sears my retinas.

"Aww, come on, Feisty One, I've got a present for you." I groan at that voice, wishing it was all just a vicious nightmare. The douchebag from the pool lounger. Cracking an eye, I glare at his well-rested boyish charm.

"Fuck off. I'm not in the mood," I scowl. He merely laughs.

"Suppose you don't want this then?" Lifting an orange pill bottle, one of my own I recognize, he rattles the two pills sitting in the bottom. I lurch upright, almost headbutting him in the face. Trying to snatch the bottle, he's fast to jerk it aside, playfulness dancing in his features. His shock of auburn hair seems brighter today, a stunning correlation to the gleam in his eyes.

"Na ah, you need to earn it," he singsongs. My walls instantly shut down. Suddenly, not even Jazzie could convince me to care less about selling a piece of my soul for a temporary high. It isn't me who would suffer the consequences, but all of those around me. Crossing my arms, a baggy vest rubs against my nipples, a pair of boxers snuggly fitting around my ass. Wait, who the fuck dressed me while I was passed out? My eyes drop to the hideous, raised scar on my forearm at the same time his do, and I'm quick to hide my arms beneath the covers. Luckily, he doesn't ask the question passing through his features.

"Breakfast is on the table. We've got a full day ahead before you get these," he shakes the pill bottle again. A noose around my neck, firmly attached to a leash. The rattle lasts in my head long after he's skipped, *literally skipped*, out of the room, echoing around the dullness of my senses. Who am I kidding? At this point, there isn't much I haven't done in the name of embarrassing myself and claiming back my meds.

Breakfast, as the douchebag called it, is a feast fit for the frat house. He's sitting at the top end of the table, alongside all those they deem worthy enough to join. Unsurprisingly, there is no spare seat for me.

"Right here, baby." He pushes back to pat his thigh. You've got to be kidding me.

"Go to hell," I scowl, turning for the main door. Hands grab me instantly, the scraping of chairs drowning out my screams as every minion who recently sat quietly eating now drags me towards the head of the table. I'm no match for their strength, but that doesn't stop me fighting back with Jazzie mentally cheering me on. My limbs flail wildly until I'm ultimately dumped on his lap. The man in question is grinning as widely as

Jazzie, who appears leaning across his shoulders. Perhaps I should behave to get my pills back.

*I know you feel that bulge as much as I do,* Jazzie winks.

"There. That's not so bad, is it?" The douchebag chuckles to his comrades on either side. Ezra is glaring at me with such disdain I can practically taste it. On the other side, a male sits silently, as if nothing exists except his bowl of fruit, yogurt, and granola. The guy caging me pulls a similar version my way, leaving the platters of steaming freshly baked goods down the other end of the table.

"Eat up," Ezra barks. I flip him off. A deep vibration resonates against my lower back. Apparently, I'm amusing my captor.

"Or don't," he leans forward to breathe into my ear. "Your insolence is the quickest way to make me rock hard." I balk, making a move to flee. The minions, who have remained stationary at his back, step forward to forcefully hold me in place. Hands pin my wrists beside his thighs, the vest and boxers being pulled in all the wrong directions. Reaching around me, a spoonful of what I can only describe as rabbit food is lifted towards my mouth.

"Open wide like a good girl, and I might fill you with something else."

"*Promises, promises,*" Jazzie muses. She settles into Ezra's lap across the table, picking up a strawberry. She only pauses long enough to spit her gum across the table into Senior Stoic's bowl and then pops it into her mouth. I watch her in real time, my eyes unfocusing from those glaring my way. I'm insane. Clinically undeniably insane.

"*The best of us are,*" she smirks. At the same time, the spoon is nudged against my lips. Once, twice. Persistently knocking. Jazzie winks again, a wicked gleam in her eyes. Watching, waiting. I can hear her thoughts loud and clear. Maybe I am insane, but I reckon the best protagonists are. Opening my mouth, the spoon glides in effortlessly. Muesli and bark scrape my tongue, incredibly dry and completely tasteless.

"That's it, Feisty One," he praises, stroking my hair. The hands at my wrists relax, and my mouth clamps down around the spoon. *Game on.* Jerking my chin violently, the metal is torn from his grip. I don't bother spitting it out, spinning before the douchebag can preempt my next move. Before he can foresee the spoon handle being thrust into his eye with a move, I usually reserve for blowjobs. My fingers are in his crotch next, grabbing for whatever comes to hand first. Squeezing, twisting, yanking. He squeals like a pig in a butcher shop, and I don't wait around to see if I've done any lasting damage.

Flanked by Jazzie, I wriggle through the minion's grabby hands. The assault of my own mind blurs within the hollers of those scrambling for my agile body, but I'm too busy ducking, skidding across the floor to where Jazzie is beckoning me towards the door. Sweet freedom lies beyond, a paved walkway between luscious green grass. The perfectly smooth tarmac and a short run back to the safety of my dorm.

Five steps from the door, my heart leaps. Three steps, and a smile spreads across my face. One step–blinding pain erupts at the back of my skull. I scream, grabbing for the hair now fisted tight in a meaty hand. Endless dark eyes glare down at me, a never-ending void that makes it impossible to settle on where to look.

"I understand you are new around here," he growls, and my stomach drops. I recognize that voice. "But it is a privilege to be invited to stay in this house. When you're given an order, you do not fight. You don't resist. You sit quietly, eat your damn breakfast, and remember your fucking manners." Using his grip on my hair, he drags me back to the center of the dining room I hadn't bothered to look at much until now.

Incredibly high ceilings seem to sparkle beyond crystal chandeliers, every wall and fixture in opulent white. Too clean for a group of young men to live in, too pristine to be used for wild parties. The only colors are soft dashes of gray in the velvet curtains and throughout the furniture. The dining table itself, now I look beyond the plates, is a slab of marble in silver and slate.

I'm held at the far end of the dining room, forced to stare at the douchebag who acts like Lord of the castle, still in his seat at the head of the table with a stupid grin on his face.

"Now, say thank you to Lucas for his kindness."

I set my jaw, my nostrils flaring. Lucas. The one I was looking for this entire time, who somehow has my med bottles and has taken great pleasure in taunting me. Beyond Lucas' back, Jazzie appears, wide eyed and shaking her head. *Don't admit defeat.* But what am I supposed to do? This isn't fiction; this is real life. One that's rapidly being flushed down the toilet, so at some point, I need to admit defeat.

"Thank you, Lucas," I grit through my teeth. I'm released so fast, I stumble into the open archway, clinging to keep myself upright. When Lucas appears before me, all auburn hair, green eyes, a shit-eating grin, and a mock bow, I let him lead me back to the bedroom, feeling my resolve drain each step of the way. Apparently, during the commotion downstairs, my backpack miraculously appeared. Sitting atop, my clothes from last night have been dried and folded neatly. Lucas wrangles his way in as I try to shut the door in his face.

"Don't get any ideas of going back to bed. First day of classes, and you've gained yourself an entourage. We leave in thirty minutes, or I'll send Kyan back up to drag you out by hair."

Lucas. Ezra. Kyan. My jailers. Throwing the clothes and Converse into my hands, Lucas shoves me into the adjoining bathroom kicking and screaming. He uses his body to hold the door closed until he manages to lock it, telling me through a slip in the wood he'll release me once I'm 'suitably dressed'. I press my forehead against the wall. All of my carefully laid out plans, the prep work I put into ensuring my first day in classes would go as smoothly as possible...wasted.

"What the fuck has my life become?" I quietly groan to Jazzie. When I hunt for her, she's reclined in the jacuzzi bathtub.

"*Quite an adventure, I'd say,*" she winks for the last time, disappearing beneath a layer of imaginary bubbles. Well, I can't argue with that.

Four years ago.

*T*he clink of the cell door closing echoes long after the guard with lingering eyes has abandoned me here. I can't turn around, unprepared to look upon the room I'll be trapped in for the next two years.

"Staring at it isn't going to open it," a voice drawls. As I take a deep breath, steeling myself, I summon the courage to face my new reality. Slowly turning around, I'm greeted by a sight which causes me to shiver.

The room is dimly lit, with pale yellow walls that have succumbed to years of neglect. The air is thick with the scent of despair and unwashed bodies. Cold *metal bars stretch across the window, casting eerie shadows on the stained linoleum floor. A single flickering fluorescent light hangs from the ceiling, its feeble glow barely illuminating the cramped space.*

*I glance at my new roommate, a girl who pulses with hostility like a thunderous cloud. Jet-black hair cascades over one eye and a piercing blue gaze that could freeze hell itself, she sits perched on her bunk, sizing me up.*

*"Fresh meat, huh?" she says with a snarl, her voice dripping with resentment. "Well, don't expect any favors from me. You're on your own here." I nod silently, picking up on her clear message: I am not welcome in this confined world we now share. Still, I try to muster up some courage.*

*"I understand," I reply softly, my voice quivering slightly. "But maybe... maybe we could find a way to coexist peacefully? It doesn't have to be like this." Her lips curl into a derisive smirk as she tilts her head mockingly.*

*"Coexist?" she scoffs. "This ain't some fairy tale, princess. You're in for a rude awakening if you think peace is possible in this hellhole." Her words cut through the air, sharp and venomous. I can feel the disdain radiating from her in heated waves. Squaring my shoulders, I decide to stand my ground.*

*"I just meant I'll stay out of your way. There's no need for added animosity." I meet her piercing gaze head-on, refusing to back down. This is my first test, and failing will only incur two years of needing to sleep with one eye open. The girl jumps down from her bunk, her four-foot-eleven height having no baring on the malice she exudes. She chuckles darkly, the sound bouncing against the cold walls.*

*"Animosity?" she repeats, her voice laced with skepticism. "Are you trying to intimidate me with big words?"*

*"What?" I frown. She takes a step forward.*

*"Do you think I'm stupid?" Her lips twist upwards. I shake my head, tripping over my words.*

*"No, I didn't–It's not like that. I was top of my English Lit class. I'm getting my masters after this."*

*"This isn't a little vacation you're going to leave unscathed. This place thrives on chaos and power struggles. Survival of the fittest, and you, Princess..." She grabs my wrist and turns it upward. "Physically or mentally,*

*you won't be leaving unscathed. How's that for a big word?"* I don't have time to gasp as a utensil appears in her hand and penetrates my skin. Elbow to wrist, she carves a bloodied line with the razor-blade tip, trailing back and forth to avoid my veins. I dare not move out of fear of dislodging her trickling path, frozen watching the scarlet spill from the cut. I'm so numb, it doesn't even hurt until my roommate flicks her blade away and strides to her bunk. Then the panic sets in. My legs shake, giving out in slow motion as I bang on the cell door, screaming so loud I can't even hear it in my own ears.

Sophia, breathe. Cauterize the blood flow. *The voice is faint but sure.* I don't have time to look for the source, too focused on following her instructions. Whipping off my t-shirt, the white now thoroughly stained, I wrap it around my left elbow and pull tight. It's not enough, but it's all I've got. All I can do. My arm...my life...it's ruined. Ruined by an asshole my mom brought into our home and defended in court. I'm alone, dying in a cell. All that exists is the pool of blood at my feet and the booming cackle of my roommate rocking back and forth on her thin mattress.

## Chapter 6

"Miss Chambers!" a sharp voice wakes me from my daydream. I'm not even sure where my mind went this time, but the interactive board certainly wasn't filled with examples of transgressive and innovative forms before I spaced out. The English Lit teacher, Mrs. Patrick, taps her nails against her desk, waiting for me to acknowledge her. *Shit.* "Are you here to better your chances of impressing me with your dissertation, or is the sound of my voice merely a vice for you to ponder your life choices?"

"I-I'm sorry, I'm here for the lecture. Please continue," I mutter, shrinking back into my chair. She looks me over, not a shred of belief in her shrewd gaze. Reaching retirement age, her wispy blonde hair is trimmed short, a cane on hand for support when walking around the desk.

"See me after class," she nods once, going back to the textbook everyone else seems to be following. I struggle to withhold my groan, causing a few nearby to chuckle. I try my best after that to focus, to stay on track with jotting down notes, but without my meds–it's like trying to steer a sinking ship. Every time I think I'm on track, an iceberg of random thought causes me to swerve, and takes too long to unscramble the words in my notepad. By then, Mrs. Patrick has moved on and I have no hope.

"Did you guys hear?" a girl from the row in front whispers to her friends. Most grunt in agreement, except one who asks, "Hear what?"

"The Thorn Brothers have chosen their new pet." Flicking to a page in the back of my notepad, I jot down 'Thorn Brothers' and any more information I reckon I'll want to come back to later.

"What?!" the brunette gasps a little too loudly. "I've applied seven times!" Waiting for Mrs. Patrick to turn back around, the original gossiper nods.

"Last night, apparently. They haven't announced who it is yet." At the same moment, a pair of large pale eyes find me amongst the masses. The blood in my veins runs cold. Letty, the girl from last night, watches me intently, her expression filled with concern. I have a few choice words for her after she abandoned me in Kyan's room last night.

"They'll probably save it for the sports rally," a girl in the middle of the row sighs. "You know how they like to put on a show."

"If the newbie lasts that long," another snickers. "Screwing three men at once isn't as easy as it looks in the pornos. The last one had to take medical leave."

"There certainly isn't anything average about those brothers." A ball forms in my throat, unbeknownst to the brunette, who giggles.

"I heard Kyan got a new piercing recently–"

"That's quite enough!" Mrs. Patrick slams her cane on the desk, making us all jolt. "Do I need to hold a full detention to re-deliver this lecture?" No one speaks. We don't dare breathe. Sitting here longer than necessary when there's gossip to be unraveled sounds like a personal type of hell. Once the session recontinues, there's no way I can concentrate now. Pet, sports rally, three at once, piercing? My mind is reeling, breath quickening as Jazzie appears in the empty seat beside me.

*"Sounds like these boys sure are a handful."* Reaching across, her hand seems to guide my own as I scrawl in the back of my notepad, dully watching the words appear. *Brazilian wax needed.* The bell blares, raising a yelp from my throat. Bags are hastily packed, bodies are moving while I sit there, too heavy to lift my limbs until Mrs. Patrick looks my way, curling a gnarled finger.

My feet fly down the steps of the lecture hall, books clutched in my arms. The closer I get, the more disapproving Mrs. Patrick's eyes grow at the clothes I borrowed from Lost and Found. She should have seen how those passing by gaped when I was shimmying down the drainpipe in my denim miniskirt and the lack of panties that Lucas seemed to provide. Now, navy leggings and a long-sleeved rugby shirt cover me well enough, my blue hair thrown up in a messy bun. At least I was able to find my glasses where Ezra left them on a library bookcase.

"Does my class seem like a joke to you?" Mrs. Patrick starts, clicking the keys on her laptop as she speaks. "I know of your history, Miss Chambers. Your scholarship states you must successfully graduate, or you'll have to pay back all of the funds. Given your juvenile record and the possibility of being a college drop-out, I don't know who will employ you long enough to do so."

"I'm well aware." My voice is short, clipped. Somewhere between my inability to focus and the flutters in my chest that I can't seem to shift, my inner bitch comes out. I know of the vicious circle I'm in. I know of the precious opportunity I have, and which the Thorn Brothers seem intent on screwing up.

"So when I accepted you into my program this late in the year, I'd presumed you'd be most eager to absorb what I have to teach you. I'm your last chance."

"With all due respect," I lean on the desk, my words not my own. No, this is all Jazzie and whoever else is living in my head. "I am my own last chance. You relay lectures you've repeated for twenty-odd years, but I'm the one who will be cramming in the library each night to ensure I wipe that cynical look from your face."

"How dare you–" Mrs. Patrick scowls until her stern gaze floats over my shoulder. The next moment, an arm rounds my waist. I blink up at Kyan's clenched jaw, his black eyes making no effort to meet mine. Which is good, but I can't help myself from glancing south to see if I can distinguish the piercing rumor. "Mr. Thorn. Forgive me. I-I didn't realize…" Is that fear I sense? Indeed, Mrs. Patrick's face has pinkened, her posture hunched as she fights to make herself appear smaller.

"Now you do. Sophia is with us. Ensure your tone and manner reflect as such." Stunned, my feet shuffle as I'm guided from the room. Kyan releases me to snatch the books I was given and stuffs them into my backpack, which was previously slung over his shoulder. Then he eases the straps up my arms, planting it on my back. My hand flies to the side pocket, hunting for my phone, but I sigh in relief when I feel it there. Tilting my head curiously, I stare at the man standing before me in the hallway, everyone nearby giving us a wide berth. A maroon t-shirt is stretched across his firm chest, tapered jeans fitting too snuggly to not be tailored to his thick thighs.

"What did you go to juvie for?" Kyan watches me too closely, his face devoid of emotion although his tone did dip as if he was trying to be sensitive. Unfortunately, his next words revoke that notion. "You seem too… weak to have survived a place like that." I scowl, stomping my heel down on his shoe. It has no effect.

"You don't know me," I growl. This hot-and-cold routine with him is seriously starting to piss me off. Still, Kyan waits as if I might dignify him with an answer. I don't have one.

The reason I ended up in that hellhole is my sins to bear. Beyond that, how do I even start to explain being incarcerated was where I developed my coping mechanism–daydreaming? I imagined friends to comfort me post-beating from the other girls, to sit with in the yard while avoiding all others. The best way to go unnoticed. The only way to survive without any long-term damage. Although now I rely on drugs to silence the voices in my head, I don't know if I would consider myself a survivor at all.

"You no longer need to attend classes," Kyan finally changes the subject, stepping in closer. I hold firm as our chests brush, his shower gel of cedarwood drifting through me. "Lucas has given you a free pass. If you see out the semester with us, you'll pass with multiple job offers in your lap. All for the easy price of sitting in his." My mouth pops open. He can't be serious.

"I don't want a free ride. I transferred schools to earn my way through." My eyes narrow. Again, I'm met with that stoic silence, Kyan's jaw tight and eyes dead. Shoving him a step back, I raise my fist to punch him, to get any sort of reaction, but he catches my wrist too easily. Spinning us, I'm suddenly against a wall, caged in by thick biceps.

"Maybe you should be a little less aggressive and a little more grateful. You're required to join us for dinner at the manor tonight, eight o'clock sharp. If you're late, or if you try to hide, we will find you." Kyan's head dips. That jaw, that devilishly taut pussy-eating jaw, scrapes my cheek, and I swear I just came a little. His lips part, brushing across mine in a whisper of a touch before it's gone. "Word to the wise, Lucas loves a chase. If you run, he'll see hunting you as part of the game."

"I don't want any part in your stupid games," I grit my teeth and try to shove Kyan away from me. He doesn't move an inch, his scent feels too overwhelming on my senses. That man from last night who held me so gently is in there somewhere, but I swiftly remind Jazzie's voice in my mind that it's not our job to coax him back out.

"Unfortunately, you've presented yourself on a fucking platter. Lucas' will isn't as strong as mine and Ezra's." Swiftly whipping himself backward, I stumble for the second time today because of Kyan. My mind trips over itself, trying to both soothe and digest the brunt of the information Kyan has delivered. Gathering my balance, I find him halfway down the hall, students parting like the Red Sea shying away from Moses to let him through.

"I hate you!" I scream, much to the shock of those watching on. I don't care what they think. I refuse to be associated with these Thorn assholes.

"Feeling's mutual," Kyan calls back, holding up a peace sign. Then he's gone, and the bell rings for the start of my next lecture. Fuck, I'm late again!

By the time lunch rolls around two classes later, I'm about ready to pass out on the table. Nursing a coffee, I lean over it as if I'm hungover. Two days without my meds; perhaps I am hungover. My fingers shake like I'm a sobering addict as the rim of the plastic cup graces my lips. It's vile. Like the equivalent of what caffeinated dog shit would taste like, but it was free.

Sitting in the cafeteria, I figured I shouldn't go crazy with my monthly food card on the first day. Luckily, it's not too busy, and I'm able to have a full table to myself to–as Mrs. Patrick put it–question my life choices. This is supposed to be my new start, and I won't let a bunch of righteous dickwads fuck it up for me. At least, not on day one.

Pulling my notepad out, I flick to the back page, glancing over the scribbled notes I made. Below, I write 'Game Plan' as a heading and underline it twice. Then I stare at it, failing to come up with anything realistic. Murder is out, running away won't work, and learning taekwondo overnight seems like a lot of effort. Glancing over to an adjacent table, I see the same girls from Mrs. Patrick's class this morning, laughing and chatting away. There's strength in numbers, and they seem to know what's going on around here much more than I do.

"I think it's time to admit, I'm going to need some friends," I sigh to myself. Jazzie appears opposite me, smiling sweetly with enthusiastic jazz hands. All a figment of my imagination. "Real friends," I drawl. When it comes to self-preservation, she always manages to be the ringleader. The loudest and most prominent. Pushing myself up, I do something I never did in juvie. I find some temporary courage and stride over to the popular girls, sliding into a free seat at the end of their table.

"Hey all, I'm Sophia. I just started here." I wave. For a millisecond, they all spin to raise brows at me, and I think I'm about to be lynched. But then they break into smiles, the volumes of their welcomes deafening. My smile wobbles. The closest, a brunette who introduces herself as Evelyn, asks a bunch of general questions which I answer evasively. Then she gives me a rundown of everyone's names, which I'll never be able to remember. Letty is in the mix.

"So, I hear there's a sports rally coming up?" I casually spin the conversation. Evelyn offers me some of her cheesy fries as everyone's faces light up.

"Oh yes! You've arrived just in time for the quarterfinals against Radley. Our basketball team here are like gods–the Thorn Brothers being the star players. Just wait until you see them," a girl called Rosie gushes. I hide my blush.

"Are they like...real brothers?" I divert my gaze to the fries. The table giggles once more.

"In the bonded sense," a redhead across the table answers. I think her name was Clara...Kerry maybe? "Their parents are extremely wealthy, but couldn't conceive themselves so they decided to adopt from a poverty-stricken orphanage. All for show, of course. Only went for one, and ended up leaving with three. Apparently, the boys wouldn't be separated. Now they stand to inherit a fortune, including this university." I choke, needing to down the shit-stirred coffee to clear my throat.

Letty just watches me knowingly and nods. "Yep. This Uni has been in their family since it was built." A shudder rolls through my entire body. I need to handle myself very carefully from now on, or it won't matter how much revision I put in. I'll be out on my ass, broke, and in debt regardless. What a way to start my adult life. Another girl with jet black hair cut into a sharp bob to accentuate the sharp lines of her face, leans forward with a cunning smile.

"If you want to get on the Thorn's radar, your best bet is to check out the bulletin board." She points across to a large board by the serving hatch. I already know I don't want to look but have to. Letty tuts, rolling her eyes.

"Don't tease the poor girl. You know she doesn't stand a chance." I conceal my frown. The bell rings, ending my short reprieve of playing catch up. The girls stand suddenly, kissing each other's cheeks goodbye and waving to me, dispersing in different directions. Letty lingers for a moment, watching the rest leave.

"Hey Sophia, about last night," she plays with a loose strand of strawberry blonde hair. "I figured taking you to Kyan's room was the safest since he's rarely at Thorn Manor. I had no idea he'd storm in and kick me out." So that's where she went. I purse my lips and say nothing as Letty looks more and more sheepish. "I hope everything was okay. When I heard the gossip this morning about their new...well, I worried..." she begins hedging around what she really wants to say. Jazzie is quick to judge, telling me all sorts of heinous ways I can use plastic cutlery to extract eyes, but I force a smile. After Kyan's warning, I need friends more than ever.

"It's fine," I wave my hand through the air. "No big deal. By the time I re-entered the bedroom, Kyan was already fast asleep. I snuck out and made it back to my dorm without antagonizing anyone else."

Letty laughs, a quick sound filled with relief.

"Oh, brill. I was worried for you all night. I'd better go, but if you fancy grabbing dinner later, a few of us girls are going into town?" I keep the smile plastered on my face.

"Ah, next time - Mrs. Patrick has given me extra coursework for disturbing her class earlier. I'll be in the library at every possible chance I get."

"That bitch!" Letty's jaw drops. I shrug to hide the way I've begun chewing on the inside of my cheek. Perhaps I shouldn't be so eager to start rumors about my tutors, but the alternative was to admit I've been commanded to spend time in the Thorn's company, and even if I hadn't, I can't afford to eat off campus anyway. Being messaged through her smartwatch, Letty balks. Drawing me in for a quick hug, she grabs her bag and leaves, promising to catch up properly with me soon.

Once the coast is mostly clear, bar the dinner ladies, I slink over to that bulletin board. Around the outside are the type of flyers one would expect, cheerleading try-outs, upcoming dances, charity events, and apprenticeship opportunities. But smack bam in the center, taking president over everything else, is a poster for 'The Thorn Pet Internship.'

*Are you looking for an exciting opportunity? In the market for quality personal references and various job offers upon graduating? Do you take pride in your appearance?*

*Enquire below to be considered for the Thorn Pet Internship program. The successful applicant will need to live-in, obey orders, and remain enthusiastic throughout the agreed term. A decent pain threshold, tolerance for exercise, and high sex drive are essential.*

*One vacancy per semester.*

"*Well,*" Jazzie leans her head on my shoulder. "*Here I was thinking they couldn't get any more shallow.*" I feel the walls closing in, an alarm ringing between my ears. This is a legit advertisement, with a QR code to apply online. Naively, I thought the brothers were just messing around, seeing how far they could push me before I went feral. Testing my limits as the new girl, or trying to scare me into running for the hills on my first day. But this... This is bigger than I ever expected, and something I don't have the time or patience to be a part of.

The shutters over the serving hatch slam closed, jerking me back to the present, where I'm undecidedly late for class–again. But as my feet start moving, my backpack heavy on my shoulders, I already know it's pointless. I wouldn't be able to concentrate now anyway, and I don't want to give anymore professors the wrong idea about me on my first day. So as much as I hate to use '*Lucas' free pass,*' I enter the hallway and stride in the opposite direction of where I'm supposed to be.

# Chapter 7

The manor looms before me like a monument of past sins, its whitewashed walls a façade to anyone who doesn't know better. It's three masters waiting inside, holding my future in their grasp. I wish I hadn't read the billboard. I wish my mind would have blocked out the trepidation I've felt all afternoon while trying to lose myself in a book. Not even reading helped. The Thorn Brothers are looking for a new pet, and I've done the one thing I swore not to. Drawn attention to myself. My heart hammers against my ribcage, a prisoner trying to escape. I've only been here two days, but Thorn Manor feels like the inevitable conclusion to a hierarchy I don't know yet.

"Pull yourself together, Sophia," I mutter under my breath as I approach the porch. Jazzie is with me every step of the way. Before my knuckles can rap against the wood, the door swings open, revealing Kyan, his presence like a silent storm. His endless black eyes don't leave mine, the plummeting pit of nothingness consuming me. His nostrils flare with impatience, and I'm certain a small noise leaves my throat. It's hard to tell with the way my pulse is thudding in my ears.

Looking past his huge frame, I frown at the interior. Tall candelabras light the lobby. The still silence between us unnerving. Jazzie shares a look with me at the same time I register what's happening. An intimidation tactic: something to put me on edge. Straightening my spine, I meet his gaze with newfound determination. It seems to be enough to grant me access. Kyan guides me into the dining hall, each step of my converse echoes ominously through the vast space. Lucas is already there, looking like some sort of dark prince at the head of the table. He doesn't stand, just watches me intensely. Like I'm a sacrificial lamb brought to the slaughter. Gone is the cheerfulness to his features. Instead, a smirk lingers, but it doesn't reach his green eyes.

"Sit." His voice is a command I instantly want to refuse. Maybe I've spent too long listening to Jazzie, but I've developed quite a stubborn streak when it comes to following orders. Kyan nudges me toward a chair, not roughly, but with enough force that resistance seems futile. He takes the time to tuck me in tightly against the table, directly opposite Ezra. It's no surprise he's glaring at me as if I'm a puzzle he can't solve—or doesn't want to. There's a feast laid out on the table, a mockery of hospitality, so far away from where Kyan tucks me in that I wonder if it's even meant for me.

"Lucas," I begin, but my voice sounds small, almost lost in the luxurious room. He holds up a hand, silencing me, and retrieves something from his lap—a brown envelope, worn at the edges. With deliberate slowness, he slides it across the polished wood until it stops just shy of my fingertips. It's all very theatrical and too rehearsed to be the first time he's put on this little show.

"Every semester, we choose a new Pet," he smirks. That word, the one I was hoping not to hear, curls around my mind like a wisp of smoke. This is bad. Seriously fucking bad. "A girl who belongs to us. To tease, to toy with..." His gaze flickers over my body, making me acutely aware of the tight-fitting sports polo and open V around the base of my throat. "...and to fuck whenever, wherever and however we like."

I swallow hard, the knot of anxiety in my stomach winding tighter. I'm no stranger to being wanted in ways that aren't exactly flattering. But this? This is different. This is a game with rules I don't understand, played by boys who see me as nothing more than a novelty. A new shiny thing to use and brake. If only I wasn't already broken.

"W-we?" I stutter, having nothing else to say when the silence stretches on, and they all keep staring at me. Lucas nods slowly.

"You heard right. We share what's ours equally, without limits. We eat together, fuck together, and reminisce together. If there's one of us, the others are never far. To keep it fair, my brothers and I take turns in choosing each semester. It just so happens, it's my turn." His smile grows wicked, two rows of impeccably straight whitened teeth gleaming like the Joker.

"Isn't that a little...sick? Brothers fucking the same girl?" The words erupt from me, a mix of fear and defiance. Jazzie is no help, her tongue hanging out like a dog in heat. Shaking my head, I try to find a different angle. "You can't just—"

"Can't we?" Ezra interrupts, his voice a gravelly sneer that sends shivers down my spine. "If we're so disgusting, why are you here, sitting at our table?"

It's true. My fingers may be wrapped around the chair beneath me as if I'm worried it'll be whipped away and I'll tumble into the abyss, but I'm still sitting here. Teetering on the edge of a precipice I didn't even see coming. I thought I wanted to lay low, to be ignored. But the truth is, and it always has been, I'm so incredibly lonely.

Lucas, Kyan, Ezra—they're offering a twisted sense of belonging that I should despise, but what if I crave the dark allure of their world? A world where Jazzie's whispers of courage have no power, where my past doesn't matter because I'm nothing but their plaything.

"Read the contract, Sophia," Lucas says, his voice a tender caress that belies the steel underneath. "This could be everything you never knew you needed."

I look down at the stack of paper, the words blurring as I try to comprehend the gravity of what's being asked of me. What's being offered. They want to own me, control me. And the most terrifying thing? A tiny, traitorous part of me is considering it.

Gingerly touching the top page, I turn it over and force myself to focus. Words are safe, they're steady—but not when they hold your immediate future in their grasp. Instead of feeling like a release, the weight of the contract in my hands is like a millstone around my neck, dragging me downwards. Jazzie's voice buzzes in my ear, a distant static which barely registers over the thumping of my heart. It's ludicrous, the demands printed in crisp black ink before me.

"You're seriously going to take me to court if I don't 'douche twice a week'?" My voice quivers, the absurdity of it all threatening to unleash a hysteria I can barely contain. Holy shit, if my heart goes any faster, I'll be spiraling into a panic attack before I can get somewhere private. Lucas leans back, his chair scraping softly against the floor, and the sound reverberates through the tense air.

"The contract isn't intended to be lawfully binding or to force you into anything you don't want to do." His bright green eyes hold mine, steady and unblinking. "Its purpose is to provide guidelines, so we all know where we stand. Besides, anything from section four onwards was added at the request of previous pets," he shrugs.

Surprise flickers within me, mingling with a creeping unease. Previous pets? The thought twists in my gut, a reminder that I'm not the first to be ensnared by their game. Were the rest as hesitant? Did they fight against the cage closing in on them? Dropping my gaze past section four, it would seem not. That's where the really dark and twisted fantasies come to life. There's a whole section on which bindings are safe to be restrained and gagged in a forest setting, and worryingly–thorny vines are noted as one of those approved.

"Give me time," I state, folding my arms to hide the tremble in my fingers. "I need to think." My gaze skitters away, unwilling to meet theirs any longer. "And to think clearly, I need my meds back. I know you have the stash which was stolen from my dorm."

There's a flicker of a smile on Lucas' lips, knowing and smug. He reaches into his pocket, and I hear the familiar rattle of pills before he places a bottle on the table. Seven pills stare back at me, a countdown to an ultimatum I never asked for. "You have until these run out to decide. After that, the decision will be taken out of your hands." His smirk is a blade, sharp and threatening.

"I thought you weren't going to make me do anything I didn't want," I scoff, the taste of bitterness on my tongue.

Ezra's voice cuts through the standoff, gravelly and certain. "Oh, you want us, Feisty One. You're just intent on fighting it for as long as possible."

Heat creeps up my neck, staining my cheeks with a telltale blush. *Stand up, Sophia. Leave.* Jazzie's command is a lifeline. Pushing back my chair, I rise, my legs shaky but determined. I need to escape, breathe, think without their predatory stares dissecting my every move.

"Fine," I manage, my voice steadier than I feel. "I'll consider it, on one condition." I expect their immediate refusal, but Lucas leans forward, seeming even more intrigued. "No one knows you've asked this of me. Should I refuse, I don't want any association with any of you. Not in my schoolwork, not with possible new friends. I reserve the right to walk away without being tainted by any of you." My eyes settle on Lucas' for a final moment before I grab the contract, turn and stride away. The room seems to close in around me, each step a victory and a defeat. They've gotten inside my head, under my skin. And damn them, a part of me is enjoying the dangerous dance they're leading. But I won't give in—not yet, maybe not ever.

Kyan moves around me, his steps silent, a predator's grace in his stride. He leads the way, and I follow, feeling the weight of their stares on my back. The cool wood of the door looms in front of us, and for a moment, freedom feels within reach. When he doesn't make a move to open it, I outstretch my arm, fingers grazing the handle.

"Wait." Kyan's hand suddenly clamps around my wrist. His other presses flat against the surface next to my head, effectively caging me in. My breath catches, the air in my lungs turning to ice.

"Just in case you need a preview of what being our pet means," he breathes, his voice low and laced with promise. His lips crash onto mine, tilting my world on its axis. The kiss is raw and bruising, stealing my breath and thoughts. His hand threads through my hair, pulling me closer until every line, every curve of our bodies melds into one. A tiny whimper escapes my lips, swallowed by his demanding mouth.

His fingers trace a path down my side, teasing the hem of my shirt, sending shivers coursing through me. I fight to pull away, to regain control, but his grip tightens in an unspoken warning.

He claims my thoughts, overwhelming my instincts with his own. Feral, consuming. My mind screams at me to push him away, but my body betrays me, melting into the heat of his touch. The shock of metal against my tongue pulls a gasp from me as I discover the cold glint of his tongue piercing. A thrill courses through me, pooling low in my belly.

Kyan's hands roam with possessive intent, branding me with every caress. I can't think, can't breathe; I'm drowning in sensation and a twisted kind of desire that should terrify me. His scent, a mix of spice and leather, fills my senses, intoxicating me further.

Abruptly, his mouth is torn from mine. Reality slams back as the door swings open, and I stumble backward, the chilled night air a stark contrast to the heat of Kyan's body. His hand snakes out, catching my waist and steadying me just long enough to confirm I won't fall.

"Consider that your first taste," he murmurs, his breath hot against my ear. Then I'm released, the door slamming behind me with a finality which echoes around the porch. None of which happened before I saw Kyan's walls come crashing back down, a barrier to keep me and everyone else out.

Regardless, I'm left panting, heart racing, a confusing mix of anger and arousal churning within me.

"Wow, looks like you got much more than you bargained for," Jazzie's voice is thick with sarcasm, coming from the shadows of the porch swing. My cheeks burn with humiliation and something darker, something I'm afraid to name. I draw in a shaky breath, trying to calm the tempest inside me. I can still feel Kyan's lips, the press of his body, the unspoken threat and promise mingled together.

"Shut up, Jazzie," I mutter, pushing away from the door. My legs are unsteady, my thoughts a tangle of fear and longing. As I make my way down the path, contract clutched in hand, the damp night air does nothing to cool the heat flaming between my thighs, and I curse myself for the reaction I can't control. Eager. I was too damn eager, too willing. No wonder they thought I'd be a pliable little pet to play with. Jazzie mutters her disapproval, trying to convince me there's empowerment to be found here, but her words are drowned out by the thunderous realization of the choice still ahead of me. I'm insulted, frustrated, and more than a little aroused by the images flashing in my mind. Either way, I'm fairly certain I'm completely fucked.

# Chapter 8

The persistent hum of conversation in the canteen blends into a jarring symphony I struggle to tune out. My eyelids are heavy, my mind thick from the same vivid dreams which kept me awake all of last night. It doesn't help that my roommate didn't come home again, leaving me feeling even more vulnerable and on edge.

Those dreams have continued to play on a torturous loop behind my eyes. Hands roam my body. Tongues brushing my neck, my nipples. I subconsciously arch, biting down on my lower lip. Then there are their gazes…the way they would consume me with a single look, melt my bones to jelly. The intimacy of it all leaves me shivering upon returning to reality.

Why are they so intriguing? Or am I just that desperate for physical contact, I'll take whatever I can get.

"Are you okay, Sophia? You seem out of it," Letty asks with a furrowed brow as she nibbles on her salad. I shake myself and plaster on a smile, knowing it looks as fake as it feels.

"Yeah, just didn't sleep well." The lie rolls off my tongue with practiced ease.

"Must be this heat," another girl, Becca, chimes in, fanning herself theatrically. It doesn't take a genius to know she isn't talking about the weather. My gaze flits across the room, landing on the Thorn Brothers. Lucas leans against a pillar, his smirk suggesting he knows every secret tucked beneath my facade. He wriggles his fingers at me. Kyan is somewhere in the periphery, his attention coming and going like the tide. But Ezra—Ezra is close. Too close. Laughter rolls off him as he flirts with a blonde who's practically whimpering under his touch on her arm.

"Looks like the Thorns are on the prowl today," Letty says with a roll of her eyes.

"Let them prowl," I murmur, even as their presence causes something to coil tightly in my chest. I feel Ezra's gaze flickering over to me, igniting the air between us with silent challenge. I will not rise to the bait. "Must be the heat," I agree, turning my back on them all. The heat of those assholes surveying the canteen like lions on the prowl. We're just gazelles in their eyes, and at Waversea, it's always open season.

More women are drooling rather than eating, craning their necks to be noticed. Although, none of them are. Just last night, these brothers were propositioning me, and now they're hanging around, not letting me think straight. And they know exactly what they're doing.

Idle conversation continues between the girls I've claimed as my friends-to-be, but I can't pay attention to any of it. I can sense Ezra getting closer, prowling for fresh meat. Soon enough, his booming laughter is emanating from our table. It's an insult to my ears, coming from the Thorn Brother, who refuses to acknowledge me beyond a glare and a growl.

*Maybe if you hadn't tried to fuck him against the library shelves, he might have been more open with you,* Jazzie murmurs in my ears. I drop my fork, giving up on my cheesy fries.

"You did that!" I whisper shout down into my own cleavage. The conversation around me stalls.

"Who did what, Sophia?" Letty frowns at me. I blush, keeping my eyes averted.

"Sorry, nothing. I forgot I need to…" I don't waste time trying to think up a lie they won't believe. Standing, I gather my tray, hastily throwing my napkin and cutlery on it. My oversized college sweater feels too heavy, my leggings too hot in the crotch area. Seriously, fuck these guys. Spinning and walking before my mind has caught up with me, I misstep, catching my converse on the wooden seat of the bench, and the world tilts in slow motion. The refillable cup of soda teeters dangerously on my tray before it cascades over the edge, its contents splashing across the front of Ezra's jeans, right over his crotch.

"Shit!" I gasp, heat rushing to my cheeks as I fumble for the napkins. My hand shakes as I reach out to dab at the darkening stain, but his grip is iron-tight as he seizes my wrist.

"Leave it," Ezra growls, the sound low and animalistic, sending shivers down my spine. His eyes are thunderclouds, promising a storm I know I'll pay for later. Why does it always have to be him?

"Sorry, I didn't mean—" My voice trails off into nothing as he releases me and stalks away, leaving me standing there, heart hammering like it's trying to break free. "I didn't know you were there?!" I try to placate him, but it's no use. He's already marched away, shoulders bunched and hands fisted.

"Talk about bad luck," Becca mutters, the words distant, drowned out by the blood pounding in my ears. Fucking hell. Why can't I have one day without incident? Throwing my tray onto the table, I seek out Letty. Her mouth is wide open but upon seeing the tears gathering in my eyes, she quickly stands.

"It's okay. It's going to be fine," she soothes, picking spaghetti from my oversized sweater. Placing the empty cup upright amongst the soda spilled all over my tray, she looks over my shoulder and flinches. That's the only warning I have as a sickening squelch slaps me in the back of the head. The sensation of wetness sliding down my neck instantly follows. Gasps ring around us as I reach back, fingers coming away coated in tomato sauce and noodles. Ezra's parting gift—a handful of spaghetti and a pair of gleeful blue eyes watching me from across the canteen.

"Son of a—" I bite back the rest of the curse, squeezing my eyes shut. Laughter erupts from a corner of the canteen, but I don't need to open my eyes to know its source. Ezra's mirth is a knife twisting in my gut.

"Hey, ignore him. He's just being an ass," Letty reassures, but her words are hollow.

"You know, they say when a boy bullies you, it's because he likes you," Becca bobs her brows. I see red.

"Shut up, Becca," I snap. "Whose abusive fucking logic thinks bullying is akin to flirting?" The mirth around the table dies an instant death. I stand there, clenching my nails into my palms, stinking of tomato and onion, refusing to give anyone the satisfaction of seeing me crumble. Because, despite the ghosts that haunt me, the panic that claws at my throat, and the hallucinations that offer false comfort—I will not let the Thorn Brothers, of all people, see me falter.

Frustration coils around the tendrils of my sleep-deprived mind. Ezra's arms bulge as he confidently crosses them over his white tight-fitting t-shirt, which appears all too clean. Ignoring the ghost of his warning glare and Jazzie's encouragement in my mind, I snatch a shiny red apple from Becca's tray. My heart races as I hurl it with surprising accuracy at Ezra's annoyingly smug face. The air around me goes silent, no one daring to inhale too sharply. I've never had a time-moving-slowly moment until right now, my heart hammering against my rib cage. The apple sails through the air, and just before it connects with his face, Ezra catches it with an impressive, almost nonchalant sweep of his arm. He takes a bite out of it, maintaining eye contact with me.

"Nice try," he mouths, twisting on his heel and throwing the apple further down the crowded canteen. It collides with a mountainous guy who looks like a beast made of hair and anger. If he's our age, he must live on a diet of steroids and crusted bread. He turns gradually, breathing through his teeth.

"Who the fuck…" his question trails off as close to a hundred students shift. Every single one of them, even those sitting at my table, is pointing an accusing finger directly at me.

"Apparently, the new girl has a death wish," Ezra shrugs, strolling across the space to pat the Monster Man on the shoulder. The other Thorn Brothers chuckle behind their hands, their faces alight with amusement, and that's when I realize no one here is on my side. Not in this canteen, not on campus. Not in the entire world. The Monster Man's eyes narrow into slits as they land on me, standing there with remnants of spaghetti still clinging to my hair.

*Uh-oh*, Jazzie whispers in my ear, her presence a trivial comforting reminder of my own courage. *This isn't going to end well.*

As if on cue, Monster Man twists like an Olympian shot-putter, vaulting his entire tray across the canteen. I duck beneath the plastic, catching the remnants of his chocolate milkshake and fries with my face. The rest of it has splattered a trail between us, covering those who happened to be sitting in the way. Suddenly, the entire canteen erupts into a chaotic food fight. Students, fueled by pent-up energy, launch their lunches at each other with wild abandon. Laughter and squeals fill the room as plates become makeshift shields and weapons. I grab the closest tray, crouching and covering my face as I creep beneath the table. A hand grabs my arm, dragging me back out.

"Oh, I don't think so," Lucas laughs menacingly. As per usual, there's a playful glint in his green eyes. "You started this mess. You don't get to wriggle out of it." Planting an orange in my head, Lucas makes a dramatic show of moving my arm and forcing me to throw it at Kyan's chest. The man in question shifts his dark, endless gaze and smiles. Not the warm, sweet kind, but the sort of smile which makes the hair on the back of my neck stand on end.

"It wasn't me?!" I shout, dodging a flying sandwich. I doubt he hears me.

The canteen is bustling with the echoes of laughter, shouts, and squeals as the food fight takes on a new level of mess. Lucas keeps his hold on my arm, although it isn't tight. Pulling me to follow him, my sneakers skid through pasta sauces and flecks of grated cheese.

"Duck!" Lucas laughs as a series of fried chicken legs batter my body like bullets. The perpetrators are a group of math nerds with thick, unruly curls and even thicker rims on their glasses. They've somehow erected a fort of trays and chess boards around their benches as if they've previously discussed a battle plan for this exact situation. Those of us who weren't prepared rush from table to table, the sound of scraping chairs and hooting laughter rife. I spot Ezra through the masses, standing with Kyan and Monster Man at the serving hatch. The dinner ladies are nowhere to be seen, leaving them with all of the ammunition. I vaguely frown, wondering why Lucas is all the way over here with me instead of with his brothers. Then I quickly remember, he's an asshole, and I don't really care. Grabbing a discarded burger from a table, he drags me onwards as I shed the bun and slap the patty on the back of his neck with a satisfying thud. Tomatoes and all sorts of salad chunks rain down on us as Lucas stills and turns on me, his eyes a shade dark.

"You're begging to be punished, Feisty One," he grins. That same grin was on Kyan's face not long ago. My heartbeat thumps loudly in my ears while my eyes dart to the doorway, trying to find an escape route. Lucas notices, his fingers digging painfully into my skin now. I let out a yelp and wrench away, hoping the baguette I smacked him over the head with is enough of a distraction to run. Instead, he lunges forward, grabbing me by the waist, and tosses us both to the floor. He's rolling us beneath a table while I struggle against the weight of his muscles. Those hands I can't be free of shift, one moving north and the other going south. His grip feels like iron around my throat, while the one which grabs my pussy through my jeans is soft. Seeking, caressing. My vision blurs at the edges as I try to squirm out of his grasp but fail miserably.

"You seem intent on burning the few bridges you have," Lucas' mouth is hot beside my ears. His fingers on my jeans refuse to stop their slow circles, increasing the heat in my core.

"You–" I rasp against his hold on my throat. Lucas shifts to cup my jaw instead. "You promised you'd keep it a secret."

"Keep what a secret?" Lucas goads, watching every conflicted expression pass through my feature. The chaos in the canteen continues around us with a roar. Students are screaming and laughing, launching food in every direction. It's like a warzone out here, and I'm caught right in the middle of it. I grit my teeth as Lucas smirks.

"Us," I grind out. His smile increases, like that of someone getting exactly what he wants.

"Us," he repeats. My chest heaves against his, trying to make some room between us. He's heavy, but damn if the length of him doesn't feel good. He knows it, too, rolling his hand against me, making me wish there wasn't a barrier between those taunting fingers and my wetness. My own hands lay uselessly at my sides, clenched into fists. I'm not fighting, although I know I should. Lucas towers over me, his grin menacing with unmasked amusement as his face begins its ascent. His hand on my jaw turns soft, his thumb stroking my cheek. That simple touch sends shivers down my spine which have nothing to do with fear or discomfort. The thrill is getting to me. Lucas' lips brush mine, we share a breath. I'm wrapped up in his feel, his scent of expensive cologne, and my eyes flutter closed.

A discarded tray crashes onto the table above us. Like a dagger through the spell I was under, I shove Lucas aside and scramble my way to freedom. Someone, please throw a bucket of ice-cold water at me because this bitch needs to cool off. From floor level, this food fight has gotten seriously out of hand. I'm army crawling through layers of soggy vegetables and pudding, the smells causing my stomach to churn. Lucas attempts to grab my legs, but I kick him off, hastily pushing myself upright and running for the door. I need to get out of here.

There's no time to look back as I run through the onslaught. As if people have been waiting for me, I'm attacked with salads, pasta, everything really.

I give up trying to dodge the assaults, my attention solely on an escape. Somewhere between the adrenaline and chaos, a smile stretches across my face. Exhilaration creates an intoxicating cocktail, and for the briefest moment, flying on slippery feet with a chest that feels too light, I feel alive.

"Behind you!" a girl shrieks, laughing as she intercepts a cupcake with her tray just before it hits me in the head. The room is a war zone; a flurry of food and laughter as I weave through the madness. My foot steps over the threshold, and with a gasp of relief, I throw myself through it, directly into the Dean's Assistant, Lorna.

"Stop this at once!" Lorna grabs my arms and sets me aside. Her shrill voice cuts through the air like a knife. The canteen freezes, the disharmony silenced, every eye turning to face the Dean's assistant. She stands there, one hand clamped on my slimy wrist, her eyes scanning the room for the culprit who dared incite such mayhem.

"Who started this?" she demands, her voice devoid of humor or sympathy. By the way her fingers twitch against my skin, she already knows the answer. My heart sinks as everyone in the canteen collectively points at me once again. The weight of their judgment bears down on me. Lucas seeks me out amongst the crowd, his eyes full of concern even though his index finger is also raised. I'm going to knee him in the balls next time he corners me.

"Congratulations, Miss Chambers," Lorna huffs, her tone dripping with sarcasm. "For the second time this week, I'd like to welcome you to my office."

# Chapter 9

Setting the final plate back in its cabinet, I wipe my forehead with the back of my head. Three days of being the dinner ladies' pot wash during my lunch breaks wasn't as bad a punishment as I had expected for unknowingly instigating a food fight. And after the counseling session Lorna sprung upon me, involving a series of breathing and trust exercises, I was more than happy to take whatever punishment she saw fit just to get out of her office.

I haven't seen much of anyone since then, but more because I've been avoiding people where possible. I sit in the back of the class, I study in the library until closing. I'm convinced my roommate is a ghost since she never comes back when I'm around. All in all, I could quite happily go the rest of the semester like this, but my anxiety about seeing the Thorn Brothers has been sky-high and I'm down to my last pill. One I'm saving for emergencies.

I've tried to read the contract, but every time, my throat constricts, my core flutters, and I become all too aware how easy it would be to say yes. Let them win. Let them have their way with me, and as clause twelve states, I would graduate with honors. Then what? I'm in the real world without having worked for my qualification, running the risk of losing my dream job. I slam the cabinet door closed and exhale. Why did they have to choose me?

Tossing my yellow gloves on the side, I stare out the window, watching students run ahead of the imminent bell. Everyone is so carefree. Their biggest worries are pop quizzes, and party outfits–menial drama. Then there's me, whose worries are causing her hands to shake. I sigh, leaving the kitchen far behind. Exiting the building, I turn away from where my next lecture is and head back to my dorm. There's no way I can focus whilst covered in grease and the smell of fajita Friday.

I re-emerge, showered, and scrubbed, in clothes which aren't stained and wrinkled, opting for cargo-style sweatpants with large pockets on the thighs and a t-shirt which stops just short of my belly button. It's one of my favorites, the motif of tea, books, and succulents representing me perfectly. Jazzie is standing against the hallway wall, giving me an approving look until I shrug on a thick, wool cardigan covered in frog faces.

*If it wasn't for the fact you're running away from your own dorm, I'd be somewhat impressed.* Her eyebrow tilts knowingly. I roll my eyes.

"I'm not running away," I snort, swiftly walking for the stairwell. I simply want to avoid meeting the person who I'm supposedly sharing a room with, who only appears to return when I'm absent and who steals from me. Since I'm certain my eyeliner has recently disappeared, I've started counting my hair pins, keeping a mental inventory. My pencil pot and the photo frame displaying motivational quotes are tucked away safely under my bed. It's not much in terms of personal effects, but that's all I've got.

## CHAPTER NINE

Keeping my head down, under the safety of everyone being in class, I explore the parts of campus I have yet to see. One place in particular has been catching my fancy, a place I dare not visit when occupied. I'm welcomed inside by a bubbly receptionist, the length of a swimming pool glistening beyond the glass wall at her back. Asking if I'd like a tour, I shake my head making her smile warmly.

"Take your time, look around. We have a state-of-the-art gym, a pool, and a sports arena. Many famous athletes come from Waversea and take great pride in returning to coach the next generation. Should you have any special interests, be sure to let me pass on your details." I share the kind woman's smile, although I have no idea why she would think I'm the sporty type. My woolen frog cardigan and glasses aren't typically her clientele. Still, I take the offer to be nosey and have a look around.

Passing through a metal barrier, I'm surprised to see most of the equipment is occupied. Music pumps louder as I stroll further into the gym, the heavy footfalls of those on the treadmills beating in time. An even split of men and women aid each other to bench heavy-weight bars or repeat perfected routines of squats, burpees, and the likes.

Slipping between the rowing machines, bolstered by the fact no one has even noticed I am amongst their midst, I press a hand to the glass wall. The pool below glistens invitingly, a mirror reflection of the high ceiling above with its rows of fluorescent lights. I can't hear the sound of water overlapping, but I can imagine it. Feel it. The momentary breaks of silence before plunging back beneath the surface again. I walk over to a nearby bench and sit to watch more closely. There's a woman swimming laps - her arms cutting through the water like knives and body glistening with perspiration beneath her swimsuit. She takes a deep breath at each wall before diving back in again, making small waves that lap against the floats separating the lanes. She's lost in her own world, finding the peace between the strenuous movements of her lean arms and legs.

Moving on from there, I wander into what appears to be an arena. I'm peering around in awe, distracted by the walkway of plaques honoring famous athletes who have trained here. Some faces are familiar, others not so much. I've almost stepped out into the center of the open space when the bouncing of a ball jolts me back to reality. Forcing myself to remain in the shadows of the bleachers, I swallow my gasp. All three brothers are here, in the midst of basketball training with the rest of their team. I recognize some from the first morning I awoke in Thorn Manor. I should turn and run before they see me, but Jazzie appears, sitting on the bleacher beside my head.

*Remember what Kyan said*, she smiles down at me, doing her best brooding man impression. *Lucas loves a chase. If you run, he'll see hunting you as part of the game.* I shudder, shifting my gaze back to the court.

Yellow and black jerseys hang from their brawny bodies, the elongated armholes giving glimpses of their solid chests when they twist and duck side to side. Somehow, the baggy shorts add to the allure, their calves and biceps equally rippling with muscle. Sweat beads from their brows, slicking their hair but not at all dampening the lithe way they move. Surprisingly agile in Air Jordans, I soon realize it's the three of them against all others.

Kyan bounces the ball between open legs for Ezra to retrieve on the other side. His messy blond hair is pulled back into a small bun, a smile on his face I've yet to see. Dribbling along the court, Lucas is waiting lazily beneath the net, examining his nails. A shrill whistle escapes Ezra, the ball leaving his hand one last time. Lucas jolts forward with the finesse of a large cat, pouncing to catch the ball and throw it in the same jump. It swivels the hoop, dropping south to declare their victory before Lucas has even landed.

His brothers are on him in an instant, scuffing up his hair, tickling, play fighting, laughing. The display rocks the perception I had of the controlling assholes, bringing a heavy dose of uncertainty with it. I shouldn't be here, creeping around in the shadows. Within moments, the rest of the team dives on their backs, and it becomes a sweaty mosh pit of fist bump. Okay yeah, time to go. I slide my feet backward, not turning my back until I'm sure I'm out of sight.

"You're not going to stay for the show, Feisty One?" Lucas yells over all the noise. Everyone else goes silent at my back and I freeze. "We were just about to all get naked and shower off. Wouldn't you like to spy on that too?" The hairs on the back of my neck stand on end as I try to shrink into my cardigan. The open door is only a few meters away. This scenario is too similar to the morning I leaped up and ran from Lucas' dining table. They're fast, athletic, but I can't tear my eyes away from the door.

*Don't do it*, Jazzie warns. We both know what will happen. Like the lighting of a fuse starting a countdown, there's no way I can outrun the inevitable explosion, but my body doesn't get the memo. In the next breath, my sneaker has hit the ground and I'm speeding through the gym with my arms pumping.

Fear and adrenaline fill me as I bolt past the rowing machine, my heartbeat thumping in my ears. The music leaking through the speakers becomes my backing track, a fast-paced dance beat that muffles my panicked thoughts. My legs are like jelly as I push myself to move faster, darting between benches and equipment. As I reach the metal barrier, a single word screams through the chaos, "Sophia!"

I can't tell who the bellow came from and instinctively glance over my shoulder. My heart stops in my chest when I see the entire basketball team taking chase, with Lucas heading the parade. His strides are long and powerful, his eyes dark and predatory. But his smirk is the most unnerving, daring me to try and escape him.

Sweat trickles down my back. Behind, the basketball team yells for those nearby to grab me. I manage to evade a series of outstretched arms, clambering over a guy on a weight bench, too distracted by not choking himself with the bar to worry about me. My sneakers hit the ground and I make it out of the automatic sliding doors, ignoring the receptionist's confused stare.

Free of the air-con, the sun slams into me with such force, I'm disorientated and turn the wrong way. An open field of lush green spans towards the woods beyond, leaving me completely exposed with nowhere to hide. My only option is to run and not look back.

"*Gorgeous place for a picnic, though,*" Jazzie appears on the ground, raising a champagne flute. I run through the center of her picnic blanket, breaking the mirage in half. My legs protest with each step, my lungs screaming for a rest. The tree line ahead grows closer in time with the hollering behind growing louder. Tears stream from beneath my glasses, cutting a path toward the roaring in my ears. There's a reason I didn't take phys ed, and why I reserve exercise for those in the books I read.

Somehow, the shadow of the trees slips over my feet as I launch myself into the woods. Pine invades my senses, the terrain uneven and slowing my progress. Braving a look back, there are too many silhouettes breaching the forest. A scream locks in my throat as I stumble, scraping my knee on the bark-littered ground, but to my credit, I'm up and moving within seconds. I need help, a distraction.

"*You rang?*" Jazzie appears before me, walking backward in full outdoor attire. Two white sticks are clutched in her hands as if we're going for a leisurely hike. I don't let up my pace, keeping my focus on the trail she carves up ahead. Her mischievous laugh drowns out the shouting of my name, the pain blossoming at my knee. Adrenaline has taken over, as has my knack for hallucinating. I follow the worn path, trusting somewhere in the back of my muddled mind, this must be the right way. Either that, or I might happen upon a hidden cave beneath tree roots and can hide out like a hobbit until the Thorn Brothers have forgotten I exist.

By some miracle, civilization appears on the far side of the wood. A tarmac road, houses, and vehicles for me to hitch a ride and get the fuck out of dodge. A smile dares to stretch across my wind-beaten face, my legs starting to wobble as I hurdle over a final log and throw myself across an invisible finish line.

Pausing for only a moment, my hands rest on my thighs, the breath heaving through my chest burning too hot. Blinking to clear my foggy vision, a house sits on the other side of the road. No–not a house. A manor.

"What the fuck?!" I rasp. Jazzie crouches down so she can give me a solid thumbs up and a wink before she vanishes. My mouth drops open. That traitorous, two faced, slutty–

Arms wrap around my middle, easily lifting me from my feet. Kyan tosses me over his shoulder like I weigh nothing, while Lucas and Ezra share a grin. There's no sign of exhaustion marring their beautiful faces. Spotting a black SUV parked in the driveway, those chasing me from behind skid to a stop. The entire basketball team, barring their star players.

"Thanks for wearing her out for us, fellas," Lucas chuckles, swatting my ass. Laughter fills my ears as I'm carried towards the manor, kicking and screaming. Catching hold of the doorway, my nails dig into the wood as I promise to violently kill every fucker standing outside on the lawn before Ezra closes the door and locks me inside.

## Chapter 10

"Haven't you ever heard of consent?! Let me go, you fucking cu–"  A gag ball is stuffed into my mouth and tied at the back of my head. I continue to scream through it, wrestling against the hands pinning my wrists behind my back. Lucas stands before me, his tanned skin, glistening green eyes, and easy smirk at odds with the monster I believe him to be. His auburn hair flicks forward, tickling my own forehead when he leans down to stare directly into my eyes.

"If memory recalls, it was you who sought us out in the gym." His thumb traces my cheek, which hollows out as I try to scream through the gag. "No need to be shy about it, Feisty One. You're curious. We gave you space to adjust this week, and you came straight back. So, I propose a test run. Let us show you what it could be like. Wake up here in the morning, and if you decide you really want to leave, we'll return you back to the dorms." I immediately cast a glance at Ezra, hanging back to watch. Lucas chuckles, sidestepping to consume my gaze once more.

"Ezra will behave. I'll personally ensure it." I narrow my eyes, flaring my nostrils. There's another important aspect I thought Lucas had forgotten, but he quickly adds–"And should you decide to leave, your meds will be replaced in full. Do we have a deal?"

One evening? One night, with the three of them? It's every girl's fantasy, but Letty's words from class echo around my skull. Something about being torn in half and a new piercing. I swallow thickly. The air thickens, Lucas' stare too intense as I fight against the voices in my mind. Jazzie is screaming at me to accept, her groin gyrating all over my vision. Surprisingly, it's Kyan who leans into my ear.

"If at any point it's obvious you want to stop, we will. We're not rapists, Sophia. We're just... curious about you too." His words are a balm to the voices in my head, bringing a peaceful silence. I exhale harshly, the decision already made. If I were to walk out now, I'd always wonder. Forever long for a second chance. I'll give them my trust for one night, see what it is they want to do to me, but come tomorrow–I'm gone. I've been trapped too much in my life to walk into another cage.

My head slowly lowers into a nod. I didn't even hear the clink of metal before handcuffs clamp around my wrists. That feeling alone is enough to fill me with regret, my squirming infused with panic. Oblivious to the cold sweat washing over me, Lucas retrieves a chair from across the bedroom I've been placed in. Ezra opens the drawer of the dresser he's been leaning against, presenting a pair of scissors. I shake my head, backing into Kyan. His body is an unmovable wall as Ezra approaches, dragging the scissors across my collarbone.

"Don't move, or I might accidentally slip and repay you for humiliating me," he pauses to silently count on his fingers, "three times." Lowering the scissors, the next time I feel the cold metal, it's slipping beneath my beloved cardigan and crop top. My complaints fall on deaf ears. He cuts it clean in half before turning his attention to the cargo sweatpants. Maneuvering the scissors without nicking my underwear takes skill, and then the scissors are passed to Kyan to cut the rest of the shirt from my shoulders and along my arms.

I tense as he moves to my left side, whimpering. Pleading for them to leave my forearm covered at least. The material falls away in time with my head falling forward, resignation coursing through me as my scar is on full show. A reminder of a time I was weak. Thankfully, if anyone notices, it's not mentioned.

I'm left standing in the underwear I stupidly picked out to make me feel empowered–a hot pink lace set with black threading. A jewel hangs from where the bra connects beneath my breasts. Ezra's icy blue eyes drink me in, slowly, thoroughly. His face doesn't shift, but the hardening length in his basketball shorts is hard to ignore.

Lucas spins the chair, signaling for me to sit on it backwards. My gaze snags on his outstretched hand, a small sigh hides behind my gag. I've always been a sucker for hands–and Lucas' are beautifully veined, his palm wide, fingers long and skilled. Oh, sweet mother of cum-milk, I'm a goner.

My thighs clench as I'm shuffled forward, and lowered to straddle the chair. Kyan positions me, pushing my back inwards to tilt my ass back, hanging off the end of the seat. The Converses are pulled from my feet before my ankles are also cuffed to the chair legs. His fingers trace my calves, curling around the back of my knee, and slowly stroke my thigh until he reaches the thong stretched over my ass.

*Click.* My head shoots upright, noting the closed door before twisting to look around the empty room. Only Kyan and I remain, aside from Jazzie. She's taking the job of being our audience very seriously, sitting back in a deck chair, tub of popcorn in hand. I squeeze my eyes closed.

"It's okay, Sophia." Kyan breathes my name too softly. Gone is the man who rallied me against the wall and threatened me to play their games earlier this week. Gone is the man I could easily hate, and I kinda want him back. Anything to avoid feeling like I trust him.

# CHAPTER TEN

"They need to shower while I prep you," Kyan continues. My heart thunders so loud, I hear it through my ears. Holy shit, this is really happening. I brave a look over my shoulder, my blue eyes large and pleading. For what, I'm not sure. Wetness soaks through my thong, the anticipation driving me crazy. Kyan lifts those endless black eyes and smooths his similarly colored hair back.

"Oh, don't look at me like that. I need you to keep hating me so I don't have to regret the handprints I'm about to leave on your ass." There he is. I scowl, a rough sound emanating from my throat. "That's better," he laughs condescendingly and delivers the first spank. I jerk, choking on my gasp. The sting fades almost instantly, not meant to hurt but to shock. From then on, I face forward and wait. And wait, until I grow twitchy. A shudder rolls through my back, my groin shifting on the edge of the seat.

Suddenly, his tongue licks the seam of the thong, clit to ass and back again. Kyan sucks the material into his mouth, humming to himself. His nose nudges at my opening as he takes his time, savoring and inhaling me. That devilish tongue spears me once and then is gone, a hard slap hitting my other ass cheek. This one is slightly harder, drawing a groan from me. My pussy is throbbing, my head hazy.

The sound of a vibrator comes just before its plump head touches my clit, on the outside of the thong. That damn scrap of material barring me from the full force of tremors. I strain against the handcuffs, clawing to shift the thong aside when Kyan withdraws fully. I scream around the ball in my mouth. Not like before, where I was fighting to get away, but a beg. A shameless plea to drive me toward the orgasm tantalizing the edge of my consciousness.

"Are you going to behave?" Kyan asks from too far away. I nod. Jazzie help me, I nod like a freaking bobble head, jutting my ass back further. Resting my breasts against the soft gray suede of the backrest, Kyan thankfully resumes his position. Kneeling behind me, his full attention on stroking the clit wand along the length of me. Clit to back, over and over. Just when I get used to the rhythm, rolling my hips in time, Kyan changes pace. One finger enters me, long and steady.

"Fuck, Sophia. You're so tight," he mutters. I bite down on the ball, lost to the feeling of him adding another finger. "We're in for a real treat with you." The vibrator meets my clit this time without any barriers, sending me into an inevitable spiral. Kyan pumps his fingers, twisting them on the way out. I'm so close, too close to surrendering everything I am and letting them have their way with me. Tremors prickle at my legs, my nipples aching. Thrusting in hard, Kyan keeps his fingers still, applying pressure to my g-spot as the vibrator works its magic. I tip over the edge, waves of bliss crashing through me as Kyan's teeth sink into my ass. The harder he bites, the harder I cum.

My muffled screams fill the room, signaling for the door to open. Ezra and Lucas walk in, their muscled bodies still pebbled with water droplets. Both wearing matching navy boxers, the tight kind, they prowl forward. Kyan swiftly withdraws. I whimper at the loss of contact.

"That was quick," Ezra states blandly, as if I was being tested on my endurance. I can't summon the energy to care right now, my head slumping on the backrest. Lucas, in all his humored beauty, tugs my head up by my messy bun.

"How does our pet taste?" he quirks a brow, speaking over me. Mentally, I object to being called 'their pet', but physically I doubt I have much of a case to argue it. Kyan, beginning to exit, stops as their shoulders bump, lifting his two fingers coated in my juices. Both keep their eyes on me as Kyan's fingers enter Lucas' mouth, his lips closing tight as he cleans my evidence from his brother's fingers. I swear, I just came again.

A third spank hits me, and I see stars. Only now do I realize Kyan was going soft on me. Ezra has no such reservations. His smacks are bound to leave me red and raw, on my ass, my thighs. He hits me until Lucas barks, "That's enough." My reprieve is ruined as his fingers push into my pussy, at least three at once.

"She fucking loves it," Ezra disagrees. I can't argue. My body isn't currently my own. Only an instrument for them to pleasure and draw orgasms from. Withdrawing just as sharply, Ezra nudges rather than hits me this time. "Spread your cheeks." I obey, rotating my cuffed hands to

# CHAPTER TEN

open my ass wider. The thong is instantly cut away. I brace myself for Ezra to continue his payback, understanding his bruised ego needs to be repaired, but instead–he and Lucas switch positions.

Everywhere Ezra lashed me, Lucas' fingers stroke. Soothing away the pain, tenderly replacing it with a loving caress. I continue to hold my ass, presenting myself to his every whim. Ezra stops before me, gripping my chin in one hand and releasing the gag with the other. My jaw clicks as I stretch my mouth, licking my dry lips to regain feeling. Without releasing my chin, Ezra tugs his cock free of his boxers. It juts right in front of my face. Holy hell. He was impressive when I saw him half-hard last time, but now…he's thicker than I could have imagined.

"Bite me, and I'll fucking destroy your ass," is his only instruction before shoving his cock into the back of my throat.

"*Well, now you're going to have to do it!*" Jazzie cries, appearing too close. I shake her out of my sight. Holding himself deep, Ezra waits to the point of asphyxiation before withdrawing. I choke, gasping for breath, but he does it again too quickly. Black dots pepper my vision. I barely feel what Lucas is doing to my rear end until a lubed butt plug enters my ass. I tense, struggling to hear his soft words to relax as Ezra thrusts into my mouth. His hand has drifted to close around my throat, feeling himself enter and retract.

The men are polar opposites in their approach, but the result is the same. Even Ezra, in his forceful claiming, drives my lust higher. Like an out-of-body experience, my mind is reeling as they plug and fill my holes. The clit wand is replaced with another vibrator, this one gliding through my wetness but not entering me far enough. I squirm, wanting it all, if only just to prove I can take it. In the same way, I take Ezra's solid cock without complaint. It's become a game of stubbornness now, seeing how long it takes me to bow out. To admit defeat. To submit.

"Alright, Lucas, kick it up a notch," Ezra growls, his voice thick. His thrusts slow as Lucas' increase, the vibrator finally hitting home. I groan around Ezra. Lucas closes his mouth around my clit, sucking, licking, nipping. Everywhere I'm being touched ignites, an inferno swirling through my core that's able to tear me apart. If only–

"My–" I manage before Ezra fills my mouth. Withdrawing slowly, he tilts his head of messy blonde hair. "My nipples. Touch them, please."

"Are you begging?" Ezra asks, a trace of a smile on his lips.

"Please," I repeat. His assault on my throat is evident by the streaming from my nose and eyes behind my glasses. A mess of his creation. Grabbing my hair, Ezra drags my mouth back over the length of his cock, and when he's fully seated, my breast is freed from my bra. Fingers roll my nipple, pinching harshly–and it's exactly what we both needed.

Salty cum slickens the back of my throat as I groan, my core seizing. I cum for the vibrator, for the butt plug, for Lucas. And Ezra comes for me. The room fills with moans, with hands fisting desperately to see out the pleasure. My body shakes with the force of my climax, although Lucas doesn't relent on my clit. Not until I've orgasmed harder than I ever have in my life and my limbs go limp.

Ezra withdraws, leaving the taste of him in my mouth as I pant, "Now we're even."

"Ha!" Ezra shouts. My eyes are heavy as I drag them up his gorgeous body, his cock still as hard. "You thought it would be that easy? I haven't filled you with half as much cum as I intend to." I hide the rising panic, thinking he means now, but Ezra tucks himself back into his boxers and leaves the room. One by one, Lucas withdraws the objects still in me and attends to freeing my ankles and wrists. They scream in protest as I'm eased to my feet and stumble into Lucas' chest. Scooping me up, I'm carried into the adjoining bathroom. Kyan is waiting there, a full bubble bath at the ready.

"How did she do?" he asks Lucas as if I'm not even here. The pair of them discard the scraps of underwear that are still left clinging to my body, remove my glasses and untie my hair.

"I think she'll be a perfect fit," Lucas mutters. I'm lowered into the bath as Kyan makes his way to the door. It's only when I realize Lucas intends to do the same does my arm lash out, grabbing his hand to halt him.

"That's...that's it?"

"You want more?" his brow quirks, that smirk never fading. I blush, biting on my bottom lip.

"I thought..." The right words fail me. Fuck, now I'm going to sound beyond desperate. "I thought I would have at least you," I almost whisper. It's ridiculous to be shy now. After everything I've said, the times I've ran, Lucas hasn't wavered. He hasn't given harsh words or promised punishments. He chose me against his brother's wishes. Crouching by the tub, Lucas cups my face and places a kiss on my forehead.

"Test run, remember? I can't give you everything, or you'd have no reason to stay." His emerald green eyes twinkle as he drags himself away, rock-hard in his boxer shorts. Maybe I misjudged both him and Kyan. Not Ezra, though, he's a raging cock munch. Opening the door, Lucas gives me one last longing look, and I remember the reason I'm here in the first place.

"Lucas," I breathe, my hooded eyes struggling to stay open. It's on the end of my tongue to ask if I deserve my meds back now, but exhaustion whips me away before I get the chance.

# Chapter 11

It's not real. It's not real. I know this, repeating it to myself like a mantra, but that doesn't lessen the quivering of my limbs. Another overbearing thud bangs on the door at my back, causing me to yelp before I can cover my mouth. It's not real. They're not real. The banging grows deafening, unrelenting. My back jolts with each one and I scrunch my eyes shut. My name is being screamed through the wood. Suddenly, it stops. I know better than to feel relieved.

"Do you really think you can shut us out, Sophia?" a whisper sounds beside my ear. My eyes fly open and widen at the three silhouettes crowding me. Malicious grins consume their twisted faces, the length elongating into gruesome masks.

"Did you forget we own you now?" they all seem to laugh in one, hollow voice. A glint of metal catches my eye, three blades being produced in their hands. No, no, no. It's not real. But it feels real as chains wind around my wrists and yank my arms forward. The raised scar I can't bear to look at on the left is highlighted, but it's my right arm the figures turn their attention to.

"Let us show you just how many ways we own you," they laugh again, just as the first blade is pressed against my skin.

I wake with a pounding headache, the echoes of many unfamiliar voices bouncing around my skull.

*"Are you hungry? I'm famished."*
*"Maybe the Thorn Brothers are famished too."*
*"They could feast on us!"*
*"If only Sophia would wake the fuck up."*

"Okay! Okay! I'm up," I groan, sitting upright. No matter how horrific my nightmares become, it's always waking after them that I dread. The true reality I face is being haunted by my delusions every minute of the day, warping my mind between what I could have and what should have been.

Holding my head, I brave a look, finding the mattress filled with figures. Jazzie is in the center, being my one constant comfort, but in moments of distress, anyone can pop up. My body protests as I push myself upright, finding that I'm naked beneath the sheets. I'm not sure how or when I maneuvered from the bath to the bed, but the morning rays blinking through velvet curtains suggest I slept all night. Another day of abstinence. This one, I can already tell, is going to be a shitshow.

Sure enough, by the time I've dragged my sore ass up, dressed in whatever men's clothes I can find, and tamed my knotted hair, the boys are sitting at breakfast. Their minions, who I now recognize as the rest of the basketball team, fill the rest of the seats, leaving no room for me. Typical. Lucas gives me a shit-eating grin, pushing his chair back to pat his knee. I don't argue this time, shuffling my feet forward to drop into his lap. Helping myself to his yogurt and rabbit food, I finish the entire bowl before he leans forward to speak.

"How are you feeling today?" he asks, running a hand soothingly over my ass, causing me to tense up. I can feel his hardness pressing against me as Jazzie nudges my left arm.

"*Horny.*" She bobs her eyebrows suggestively. "*Lustful.*"

"Shit," I settle on. "Do you think I could have just one more clozapine? It would be enough to get me through the rest of the week." My question is intended for anyone who's listening, but I only seem to have Lucas' attention. My palm rests heavily on my forehead. When no one responds I force myself to look back into Lucas' piercing green eyes. He's the ringleader; the one who decided I should play their twisted games.

"Well," he begins, his signature smirk fading into a serious expression. "I suppose it depends on whether or not you're planning to stay with us." My heart sinks at the thought of being trapped here without my meds any longer. The sex, the dynamics. It's all too intense to manage when my mind is already at war with itself. Lucas strokes my neck, his words sinking in slowly, and I shoot out of his lap in an instant, fueled by rage. In my fury, I kick at the table leg and immediately regret it as pain shoots through my foot.

"They're my fucking meds. Why haven't I earned them back by now?! You promised if I rejected your proposal, I could return to the dorm with a full supply of pills. You said that!" The desperation in my voice is evident, but Lucas remains cool and composed.

"True," he concedes. "But if you choose to stay here, you must learn to cope without relying on them." My jaw drops. He can't...he's not serious.

Figures linger on the edge of my vision, stepping forward to crowd me. I can't breathe, the very air stolen from my vicinity. Unlike Jazzie, the figures leaking from my mind now aren't for mere distraction. These are the antagonists, evil silhouettes who wait on the sidelines for when I'm about to crack. Waiting for the chance to swoop in. To command me, control me.

Through it all, like a glowing beckon, I focus on the brightness of Lucas' eyes. My fingers twitch to reach out and steady myself on his broad shoulders, but they might as well be pinned to my sides. There's no use trusting the wobble in my legs either.

"I can't...I need..." The quickening rise and fall of my chest is detrimental to the tightening inside. I can't draw a full breath, yet am breathing too fast at the same time. There's not enough air, not enough time.

Vaguely, Kyan tells everyone else to leave, followed by scraping chairs and a flurry of movement. Not around me, though. Those shadows cling close, sneering in my face, anticipating my downfall. My eyes are hooded again but not from exhaustion. This is much worse.

"Sophia," my name is called from far away, the sound muffled as if I'm underwater. My arms are steadied by gentle hands, keeping me from collapsing to the ground. Blinking rapidly, I try to focus on the source of the voice–and then I see them. Green eyes, like a beacon in the darkness, calling me home. But nothing is ever that easy.

"Was I not enough for you last night?" I whimper, my question surprising even myself. It comes from a place of vulnerability, raw and exposed. Swallowing back the rising tears that accompany my words, I rephrase. "Why are you punishing me?" But it's too late, the tears come anyway. Thick streams running down my cheeks, staining my band t-shirt.

"I'm not punishing you, Feisty One," Lucas speaks softly, his touch gentle as he tucks a strand of blue hair behind my ear. His words become muffled, drowned out by the dark voices in my mind.

*Liar. He's using you because you're a slut. He wants you confused, easier to take advantage that way. A mindless sex doll for his brother fetish. You're only good for one thing.* The voices taunt me mercilessly, their venomous words echoing in my head. Jazzie tries to break through, but it's no use. She isn't loud sometimes.

"Sophia? Did you hear what I said?" Lucas' concerned frown comes back into view as I fade in and out of consciousness. In a final attempt to hold onto reality, I lift my head–but it's too heavy. Strong arms catch me before I hit the ground and the darkness takes over completely.

# Chapter 12

Three Years Ago.

*F*ire dances. Flame intertwines. The warmth casts a glow on my skin, the hideous scar spanning my left arm shunned by the shadows. Pain doesn't exist here. My manufactured heaven. The floor beneath my bare feet isn't that of my cell, but a pale marble reflecting the light dancing from the hearth. I always saw myself as a simple girl of simple means. It's ironic the world I've created for escape should drip in splendor. Stone walls adorned in rich, velvety tapestries of cerulean and gold, high ceilings lost to darkness above. But it feels homely, welcoming. A stark contrast to my cold, hostile confinement.

I walk over to a grand mahogany table adorned with food and drink. There are meats cooked to perfection, fruits glistening with dew, rich pastries, and cakes dripping with sweet syrup. A banquet fit for royalty. Guided by an unrestrained hunger brought on by countless days of prison grub, I reach out for an apple.

"Sophia," a voice calls out softly. It's strong yet soothing. Turning, I find her standing at the threshold of an enormous window overlooking an expanse of star-studded night sky. A female figure stands with the posture of confidence. Someone who knows exactly who they are and what they're about. Silver highlights trickle through her dark hair, a shade lighter than black. Hazel eyes track me, a sense of familiarity in her gaze. I've dreamt of her before. Many times.

"You're safe here," she assures me with a tender smile. I never know which version of her I'm going to get, but she flawlessly adapts to her surroundings. Today, she appears radiant in a silken robe which billows in the unseen breeze. Safe? The word echoes around my head. Words are so easy to say, but safety isn't something I've been able to feel for a very long time.

"Sophia!" my name is called again, but not from this world. I whimper, not ready to go back when a sudden weight strikes my face. My head whips to the side, tears forming in my eyes as the extravagant room leaks away. I don't know what I'm more upset about; the football which just landed a full-bodied blow to my face, or the fact my fantasy has been broken before I can see it through. Towering over me, my roommate grabs the ball and sneers.

"As if you never learn. You're an open target, and then wonder why I screw with you." The girls at her back laugh and bump shoulders, all staring down at me on the bench. I hate yard time the most. So exposed with nowhere to hide. "Hey, I'm talking to you," Thistle slaps my other cheek. Her real name is Thea, but no one is allowed to call her that.

"One of these days, you won't need to pretend the real world exists," she cackles. Rule number one of juvie, when the counselor tells you it's best to write down your 'healing journey' and keep it hidden under your bunk, don't do it.

*Leaning closer, her twisted hateful face is all I can see.* "Because I'm going to put you in a coma one of these days. The extra time will be worth it, knowing someone as pathetic as you isn't getting out of here before me."

Her friends join in with the taunting, backing up their leader. The idle insults grate on my nerves, but a certain voice speaks louder. The one from my daydream.

*They're never going to stop until you show them you're not spineless.* I sniff, holding a hand to my cheek. *You need to have some fight.* Somewhere, from the reserves of my tattered being, I manage to lift my head and glare through my tears.

"No, Thea," I drawl out her name, mustering as much venom as I can muster. A collective gasp echoes around the group, and Thistle's laughter dies immediately.

"What did you call me?" she asks, her knuckles whitening around the football.

"Sorry, I forget you're both illiterate and ignorant–Thea," I put emphasis on her name, feeling a strange mix of fear and satisfaction. Thistle hates it when I use long words. She lunges forward and punches me in the stomach. I double over in pain but manage to catch myself from falling from the bench and curling up on the ground. Putting myself in a more compromising position will rescind all the confidence I've just conjured.

"Who the fuck do you think you are?!" Thistle screams. She looks around at her friends for support, but they're all staring wide-eyed, unsure what to do. It seems they've never seen anyone stand up to Thistle before.

"Just leave me alone," I grunt out through the pain. Thistle lets out an angry huff.

"You're not worth wasting my valuable yard time over," she snaps, turning to walk away with the football. "I'll see you back in the cell, roomie."

You'll survive, *that same voice from earlier sounds. I feel her presence at my side, a lingering comfort I subconsciously lean into. Tendrils of dark hair laced with silver highlights trickle over my arms, a chin resting on my shoulder.* You have to. You've got a life to live once you get out of here.

# CHAPTER TWELVE

*"I-I don't think there's anything worth surviving for. I've got no one waiting. There's just...nothing,"* I whisper quietly. Keeping my chin ducked, my words are kept private for the one they were intended for.

*And since when have you needed a reason? You've been alone for far longer than you've been here.*

*She's right. My mom's latest boyfriend wasn't any different from all the rest. Assholes, junkies. They used her, she used them. But it wasn't until the latest that the attention was turned on me. Me–the fragile girl who hid in the attic, lost in her books and her studies. I knew from a young age I was going to become more than my roots. I'd make a life for myself and never rely on drugs to get by. Until that attic became my personal hellhole. Now look at me, in jail for defending myself, my life in shambles. No one will accept or employ me after this.*

*I'm Jazzie, by the way, and I'm going to help you. The woman, probably in her twenties, gives me a knowing look, as if she's seen the entire world and has the secret to succeeding in life sorted into a simple formula. I know she's imaginary, a figment of my desperate and fragile mind struggling to keep a grasp on reality, but I can't help my small smile. For the first time, I don't feel quite so alone. I have a friend, and I don't even need to lose myself in a daydream to find her.*

## Chapter 13

"What do you suggest?" Lucas' voice is clipped. Even before I open my eyes, I've tuned into his mood. It's unlike him to speak so harshly, and anyone who hasn't had fitful dreams of being an unworthy whore would mistake his tone for concern.

"My advice is to give her back her prescribed medication. She was given them for a reason." The second voice is unfamiliar. I fight against my eyelids to open but the blinding lights waiting on the other side make it impossible. A metallic crash causes me to flinch, my arms seizing painfully around the needles embedded in the crooks of my elbows.

"She's not going back on that shit!" Lucas shouts, clearing the fog from my mind in an instant. I hear Kyan quietly soothing him, offering to speak with the doctor outside. Great, I'm in a freaking hospital. My second least favorite place to be, after juvie.

My senses quickly catch up with my mind, the scent of lemon detergent tingling my nose. From this position, fully reclined on my back, the rigidness of a hospital gown implies I've been stripped down and changed. I briefly wonder if there were any questions about the bruises and a bite mark on my body I'd rather not have to explain.

Silence settles, the opportunity to escape lulling me back into a state of calm. It's best to find the peace where I can, focusing on my breathing and not thinking about the field day Lorna will have with this episode during our next counseling session. If I remain still, if I drift back to sleep, the rest of the world doesn't have to exist for a while longer.

"I get what this is," Ezra speaks so suddenly I flinch again. I hadn't realized he was even in the room. "Because your birth mom overdosed on hallucinogenic shit. You think you can be a savior this time." A weight sits on the edge of the mattress. Unfazed, Lucas takes my hand in his, stroking circles with his thumb. Ezra sighs from across the room. "You can't fix her."

"She's not broken. She's confused," Lucas' voice is small but steady.

"You want to undo years of trauma in one semester?" Ezra scoffs. My heart is batting around like a ping pong ball, and I'm immensely thankful no one hooked me up to a heart monitor. "You're getting married as soon as you graduate. This isn't the time to start feeling sentimental." Wait, what? Ezra moves closer, leaning over me to get Lucas' attention. "This isn't our battle to fight. I admit, she's interesting. But she's also complex, Lucas. Just let her go, and we'll pick a new pet. An easier one."

*Wow*, Jazzie immediately intervenes in my head. Or maybe that sarcastic drawl was all me. My gut sinks, a sickening feeling taking over. I can't disagree that I'm a mess no one has any business trying to help, but it doesn't lessen the hurt. Lucas, though, doesn't seem to care.

"It's my turn to choose, and I chose her. The real her–not some drugged up version. I've been on the receiving end of intoxicated affection before, and you never know if it's genuine. I need to know this time."

"Seriously, Lucas," Ezra groans. A slap sound gives me the impression he's palmed his own forehead. "You can't save the freaking world. Whatever charity case this is—"

"Call her that again," Lucas' voice has dropped, his thumb stilling on my hand. The tension is thick, making it almost impossible to pretend to still be asleep. If I weren't so nosey and wanting to continue eavesdropping, I'd have found a way to punch Ezra in the balls by now. Lucas exhales audibly, continuing his stroking over my skin. "You'll see soon enough. She's worth it, I promise."

I shift then because if I didn't twist my head to the side, I'd choke on rising emotion. I knew today would be a shitshow, but this is something else. One Thorn is fighting for me while the other thinks I'm a piece of shit he scraped off his shoe. Fan-fucking-tastic. Hands cup my cheeks, the outline of Lucas giving me enough reprieve from the bright lights to peel my eyes open.

"Hey beautiful, you're awake. Scared me for a minute there." Just like that, his easy smile is back. A rasp escapes me, my throat parched. Lucas is quick to offer a cup of water, raising the recliner bed and tilting the cup against my lips. Each of my movements are tracked by his ever-watchful green eyes, as he refuses to move out of my immediate proximity.

The room is nothing like I imagined–and not a typical hospital after all. The clinic's private room with a lone hallway window provides a high-tech bed, which Jazzie is sprawled across the foot of. Smacking the control of the personal TV, she starts yelling that she needs her daily dose of Judge Judy. I glance away, noticing a small refrigerator containing sandwiches through its glass door. There's even artwork on the walls, a mix of abstract and still-life's connected by their use of pastels. Occupying one of the large, leather armchairs in the corner, is Ezra.

"The doctor said it was just a panic attack," his icy blue eyes roll. *Just.* I find the strength to scowl at him.

"You'll receive the best care here; I'll make sure of it." Lucas adds, regaining my attention. My heart melts for the way he's looking at me.

Auburn hair flopping aside, green eyes filled with warmth. His hands are everywhere, stroking, caressing. Like he...cares.

"Your...your brothers are right," I finally manage to force past my lips. "You should pick someone...easier." A ball forms in my throat, and I look away.

The whole 'pet' idea is a stupid one anyway, but after last night–I'd be lying to say I wasn't curious. They only pleasured me with toys. I bet having their bodies, their undivided attention, is an experience I'd never forget. If I weren't me. If I were normal, I'd jump in headfirst. But I'm not what they intended. And then there's mention of a marriage?! How the hell does my life always find a way to become so messy?

Shifting, Lucas kicks off his sneakers and climbs into the wide bed beside me. The silkiness of his basketball attire allows him to slip beneath the sheet with ease, his shoulder dropping to indicate I should put my head there.

"Luckily for you," he sighs, and I can still hear the smile in his voice, "I never do as I'm told. The exact opposite, in fact." Ezra grunts in agreement. I swallow thickly, hunting for something to say when the door opens. Kyan appears, his dark eyes meeting mine in an instant.

"Well, hey there," his features instantly relaxing. Crossing the room on long strides, Kyan proceeds to scuff up my hair. "Back in the land of the living?"

"It's debatable," I snort, giving Jazzie a side glance. She's given up on the TV and is now in the hall, attacking a vending machine. At the rate I'm going, I wouldn't be surprised if the Thorn Brothers were all part of my delusions and I'm actually locked in an institution somewhere. At least Kyan blocks my view of Ezra while his fingers linger in my blue hair for a few seconds longer. As always, I can't decipher what is lurking within his fathomless dark eyes.

"How about when you're ready, we get out of here and go for a swim?" he tilts his head. I almost smile, already imagining how diving into the serene blue could wash away my worries for a while. The voices don't seem to follow me when I'm underwater. But it's the resurfacing, it's everything hitting me at once, which is the issue.

"Ugh, I can't afford to fall behind with classes any further. If I'm too late to get back, I have to study at the very least." Kyan frowns, withdrawing his hand as if I've insulted him.

"You're with us now, you don't need–"

"Of course," Lucas interrupts, inclining his head with an air of authority. "Studying it is. You're one of us now." I catch how Lucas corrects Kyan's initial response, but I don't comment. Not when Lucas heaves up my heavy bag of textbooks which was tucked beside the bed, almost as if he knew I would want to keep myself distracted. Kyan doesn't object further, instead quietly fetching an overbed table and helping Lucas to set up my makeshift study space. He even brings out his own MacBook, ready for use.

I merely sit there, still adjusting to my new reality, as I watch the pair of them fuss. I don't dare mention I haven't officially signed their contract yet, but it seems redundant at this point. I'm coming to realize Lucas typically gets his own way or will use his charm until he does. I know I'm not what they bargained for, but who am I to keep arguing Lucas' choice? He's chosen me. That in itself gives me something worth trying to live up to. I've fully decided not to extend that curtsey to Ezra until the screech of chair legs finally slices through the room. Ezra drags his armchair to the side of the bed, propping his sneakers up on the edge of the mattress without hesitation. His face is grave as he points to the textbook placed in my hands and sighs.

"Come on then," he says sternly. "Read through to section three and take thorough notes. I'll be quizzing you later, and I won't go easy." Despite his tough approach, I can see genuine concern in his eyes when he looks at the man fluffing my pillow. It all clicks into place, then. Whether Ezra agrees with Lucas or not, he will honor their agreement. They're bonded brothers, and that must be what having family means.

## Chapter 14

It turns out, the swim was non-negotiable. We stayed at the clinic until the sun began to set, and by the time we left, I didn't have half as many worries to wash away. Ezra was true to his word, testing me vigorously and marking my answers harsher than any exam board would–but it helped. In fact, I pushed myself harder just to prove him wrong, while Lucas typed up extra notes and Kyan supplied us with endless coffee refills and vending machine snacks. After a while, I even forgot Jazzie was still watching in the background.

Floating on my back, I drift gently in the waves while the others competitively swim lengths. The four of us have the entire pool to ourselves, which I'm sure isn't a coincidence. Glass cut-outs span the domed ceiling, allowing for the starry night to leak inside. Around the edge of the dome, LED strip lights have been dimmed. The main source of light bleeds from the lavish locker rooms where our clothes, bags, and the horde of my delusions are waiting.

From the edge of my peripheral vision, Kyan is climbing the ladder to the tallest diving board–again. I've decided he's the adrenaline junkie of the group, continuously throwing himself into the air with a whoop or a holler. He twists without the need to try, his flawless body rotating mid-air until his hands join into an arrow to enter the water with minimal splash.

"Show off," I mutter and smirk. Not more than a few moments later, hands drag me beneath the surface. I buck, bubbles streaming from my mouth as I scream. My assailant manages to stay out of sight by the ink spill my darkened blue hair creates around my face. Kicking upwards, I manage to inhale a full breath before those hands are on me again. Tugging on my feet, another set of arms band around my middle. A solid erection presses against the ass of my red bikini, and a third frees my breasts. They're all here, circling me like sharks. I can't fight, and in all honesty–I don't try that hard.

I'm tugged backward, my lungs beginning to burn for air as we reach the edge of the pool, and I'm allowed to surface. My feet scrape the steps until I'm drawn into Kyan's lap, his arms around my middle acting as a restraint. Ezra pops up from the water, Lucas at his side. The pair of them stride in slow motion style with rivets of water dripping down their abs. They know what they're doing. Taunting me, seducing me.

I forget all about my exposed breasts until Lucas cups one, causing me to gasp. My nipple pebbles in his hand, Ezra rolling the other sharply between his fingers. Like sugar and spice, yet again, their approaches are polar opposites, but have the same result. One which Kyan discovers when his hand dips into my bikini bottoms.

"So wet," he purred, lazily stroking circles around my center.

"Well, yeah," I reply too breathily. "We're in a swimming pool." All three of them chuckle, but I don't care if they see me blush. Not when Kyan spreads his knees to open up my legs and shifts my bikini aside. Ezra sinks down onto his knees, ravaging my pussy with the expected vigor. Sucking my clit hard, he splays me wide open with deft fingers, his tongue traveling south to eat the wetness from my cunt. Like a man starved, his tongue is relentless. My mewls fill the pool room, bouncing around the dome ceiling. Ezra always seems to be punishing me, and I'm not complaining.

My eyes crack open to find Lucas watching. His all-seeing green eyes are fixated on my face, his hands still working my breasts into a frenzy. I buck against Kyan's hold, twisting my head into his shoulder. His face greets me there, a strained and desperate kiss passing between our lips. No matter how much these men, these brothers, give me—I need more. More pleasure, more connection. Kyan's tongue swirls in my mouth in a similar fashion to how Ezra's circles my channel, digging deeper than any man has before. Whatever he's searching for, I give to him within a minute of blissful torture. On a strangled cry, I clench, convulse, and cum on Ezra's tongue, my body only easing when he sits back and licks his lips clean.

*What are they doing to me?*

"You've been such a good girl, Feisty One," Lucas comments. His fingers trail my jaw, his thumb stroking my bruised lips. "So good, in fact, I think you've earned some cock tonight." My heart stills, a shudder running the length of my body. I'm not cold, not with Kyan's heat pressing into me as solidly as his erection, but goosebumps line my arms regardless.

"I agree," Kyan adds. "Who are you going to choose, Sophia?" His purr rumbles against my ear lobe before Kyan takes it into his mouth and playfully nibbles.

"Who, err...what?" I struggle to focus. Beyond horny and dripping wet, I couldn't care less for their mind games. "Not...all?"

"Not quite," Lucas grins wider than I've seen before. "You're not quite ready for us all yet. Choose who you'd prefer to take you this time. The others will watch." Flames ignite in my core at just the thought. I know who I want, and his cocky shit-eating grin knows it too.

"Lucas," I breathe, barely any sound coming out. Kyan doesn't hesitate, whisking me up into his arms and carrying me into the locker rooms. I catch his gaze a few times, wondering if he's pissed, and if he is—he doesn't show it. Untying the bikini straps, he strips me naked, and strokes his fingers over my hip before heading to the wooden bench. Ezra joins him there, and my eyes widen.

"Wait, you mean...here?! As in here, and now?" I ask Lucas as he casually meanders through the adjoining hallway. There's a swag to his step, a cocky attitude from being chosen first. At some point, I'll have to inform him the only reason I didn't choose Kyan was because I'm semi-scared of the piercing rumor.

"Something you should get used to rather quickly," Lucas says, reaching for my wrists. "Being our pet means we take you when we like, where we like, how we like." He pushes me a step back into the lockers, pinning my arms above my head. "Consider having the choice as a one-time courtesy. After we've fully and publicly claimed you, we won't be holding back anymore."

His mouth descends on mine, igniting a heated passion between us within an instant. I wriggle free, my palms instantly pushing against his chest, but not with any conviction. I want Lucas exactly where he is, his tongue invading my mouth and senses. I love the way he tastes; smoky and spicy, even with the scent of chlorine dripping from his auburn hair. I gather all of my strength and shove him away properly this time, panting. "Your brothers are just going to sit and watch?" I swallow hard.

"It's not like they haven't seen it all before," Lucas smirks cockily.

"I know." I duck aside when he tries to grab the back of my neck, using the droplets coating my skin to my advantage. "But this is different. If you're actually, like, entering me," I blush hotter than ever before. All three of them laugh this time, loud and unfazed. Lucas reaches for my waist, pulling himself back flush against me.

"Oh, I'm going to do much more than that to you, Feisty One," he murmurs. "And yeah, they're going to watch it all. They'll be taking notes on how to make your chest flush, what makes you scream, how beautifully you break." My knees buckle at his words, my arms wrapping around his neck of their own accord to stop me from collapsing. At the same time, Lucas' fingers thread into my wet hair, gently easing my head back.

"Open," he says, his mouth closing over mine again. His kisses are rough, as dominating as the man before me. I'm weak for him, regardless of the fight I gave. Lucas isn't the spoiled asshole I thought. Or maybe he is, but the way my body reacts to him can't be ignored. Fingers slowly play across my shoulders, down my sides to my waist, and then dip between my inner thighs, making me ache with desire.

Moments later, his fingers enter me, and I cry out in ecstasy, welcoming the rush of pleasure coursing through my body. Lifting my leg to grant access, Lucas uses his free arm beneath my ass to lift me higher, caging my body against the lockers. His thrusts become harsher. Crazed. I fight against the tremble in my body..

"Lucas," I whimper into his mouth. My kiss becomes sloppy, distracted, but Lucas naturally takes charge. He knows exactly what he's doing to me. His pace doesn't falter, his palm slamming against my clit. The friction of my back against the cool metal is breathtaking. My hands roam all over Lucas' body, feeling his muscles tense with each movement. His biceps flex, his arm pumping. My nails leave traces along his shoulder blades, his back, his neck. No patch of skin I can reach goes unmarked as I hurtle toward the blinding heat of an orgasm unlike any other.

"Do it," he encourages, and I'm only too happy to obey. As if my body was waiting for permission, trying to block out the stage fright of having two other pairs of eyes watching my every expression. Clenching around Lucas' fingers, he continues until I come back to earth. Lifting his two fingers in the air, he smirks.

"You know the drill." My eyes widen, confused who he's speaking to, until Kyan appears. Dipping his head, those endless onyx eyes remain on me as he sucks the fingers coated in my desire into his mouth. I tremble again, a whimper trapped within my throat. Lucas chuckles against my chest, his hips helping to suspend me in the air. "Sophia likes it when we clean her juices from each other, don't you, baby?"

"As long as it's not your cock," Ezra grumbles from the bench. I can't respond, and luckily, I don't have to. Kyan slinks away, and as I prepare for

Lucas to put me down, he tugs at his swim shorts for his dick to spring free. *Holy mother of veiny shafts.*

"Don't look so surprised. You choose me, remember?" Lucas bites his bottom lip playfully, stroking his dick along my pussy. Between my wetness and the rush of water droplets rolling down my heated skin, my body is ready for him. I moan, my head lolling to the side and giving him all the permission he needs.

Clamping his hands around my ass, Lucas drives into me in one harsh thrust. I scream out, instantly remembering myself. They're all watching, learning, and some stubborn voice in the back of my mind–probably Jazzie's–doesn't want me to make it easy for them. Locking my arms around his neck, I bury my face into his collarbone.

Those large hands on my ass tighten, giving Lucas enough grip as his pace increases in an attempt to dislodge me. The slapping of wet skin combines with the jingle of the lockers, but not a sound passes my lips. Not until my hair is gripped and thrust backwards. A pained hiss leaves me. I could have bet who'd be there. Ezra glares at me, his blue eyes ice cold and penetrating.

"My brother told you to flush, scream, and break for us. We don't like repeating our orders twice." *Orders*, my mind relays back. Kyan appears on Lucas' other side, the three of them shoulder to shoulder as I'm fucked, thoroughly and completely. My cunt is screaming for another release, my body trembling as Kyan's large hand slips around the base of my throat. Not squeezing, but there to deliver a message.

Regardless of who's dick is pounding inside of me, regardless of who I chose, they were all going to be my dominators tonight. All prepared to take pleasure from my suffering.

My toes curl as Lucas' mouth closes over my neck, sucking and biting. The sensation, paired with the movement of our groins slapping, is too intense; much more than anything I've ever experienced before. When I'm sure I'm going to pass out, someone's fingers seek out my clit, and I'm lost. The combination of pleasure and pain, the stroking and the biting, is enough to make me see stars explode behind my eyes. Lucas groans in time with my own, his mouth finding my ear.

"You're so close," he whispers, his teeth scraping against my earlobe. "I can feel you shaking. Are you ready to come with me, Feisty?" My body jolts against him as if I've just been electrocuted. That's all I need to tip over the edge, taking Lucas with me. I feel him swell, but any sudden questions I had of Lucas' intentions to explode inside of me are quickly diminished. His dick is whipped from me in an instant, those same fingers from my clit replacing him. Pumping two, three long digits at the same punishing pace Lucas has set, I detonate, my teeth sinking in my bottom lip.

"Scream," Ezra barks, and I obey. I call out Lucas' name again and again, as he pumps his cock and explodes all over my stomach. I barely notice, my body and legs growing numb. Tears slip from the corner of my eyes. It's all too much.

By the time I'm a jerking mess and slumping against Lucas' chest, my nails have cracked against his skin. Rivets of blood stream south.

"What a fucking mess," I sigh, too weak to care. Multiple chuckles respond, Kyan cupping my cheek.

"Welcome to a life with us," he kisses my forehead. I'm passed over, cradled in Kyan's arms and walked towards the showers. It's only when Ezra lathers up his hands and proceeds to wash me down, I realize we all have a part to play here. Outside of this shower, Ezra may act as if he hates me, but I'm his pet too. He'll care for me when it really matters, I think.

## Chapter 15

Purple highlighter in hand, my eyes skim the first draft of my essay, picking out words I've used too often. After I've finished with the purple, I'll go back in with the yellow to underline where I should add references. It's a lengthy process I've perfected to work for me, but today feels more tedious with the eyes of three Thorn Brothers staring from across the dining room.

"I've already told you, I'll be fine," I huff. In my peripheral vision, I see them all straighten in the doorway. "Go to your fancy family event. I'm just going to sit here and finish this essay before Mrs. Patrick calls me out in class again." None of them leave, so I go back to reading my handwritten work. I thought they'd have grown bored of watching me by now. Last night, one by one, I seemed to gain another addition in the bed, but I'm not complaining. The nightmares were kept at bay, and I didn't need to overdose for it.

It isn't lost on me how my recent panic attack has set them on edge, and I wouldn't class it as an extreme one. In fact, they haven't left my side since I was discharged from the clinic. What worries me the most is that I'm becoming far too comfortable with them lingering close. I fear what happens when I get to the point of being dependent on it.

Finally, they can't wait around any longer. Headlights of a car pulling up outside momentarily flash through the curtains, the beep of a horn announcing their time to loiter is up. Three impeccably pressed suits approach me, Kyan easing the highlighter from my grip.

"We've made sure the team stays elsewhere tonight. Lock the door after we've gone." His dark eyes wait for mine to lift and register his order. I purse my lips and nod. Ezra's hand whips out, gripping my chin and twisting me to face him.

"Promise us you won't do anything reckless while we're gone," he demands, his eyes locking onto mine with an intensity that leaves me feeling exposed. I manage to withhold my frustration.

"Guys, I'm a big girl. If you don't want me to feel the need to escape, stop building a cage around me." Ezra's hand instantly drops away. The horn outside blares again, more insistently this time.

"We'll be back as soon as we can, Feisty One," Lucas murmurs, his lips brushing against my cheek. The warmth of his touch sends shivers down my spine. Kyan and Ezra follow suit, each pressing a soft kiss to my cheek and forehead. I swallow hard, trying to ignore the fluttering in my chest as Ezra's mouth lingers beside my ear.

"Even big girls can act stupid. Don't get any funny ideas."

"Of course not," I smile sweetly to put him even more on edge. The boys stroll away, their muscles shifting within navy blue blazers and white collared shirts. Kyan's black hair sweeps in all directions, while Lucas' shock of auburn locks are as unruly as Ezra's wild blond nest. It doesn't matter either way. With the snug fit of their tailored slacks, no one is going to be looking above their waistbands. The front door clicks shut and despite Kyan's request, I hear the key twist in the lock. Rolling my eyes, I wait for the headlights to flash once more, signaling their departure before pulling my phone out from between my thighs.

'You ready yet?' Letty's message pops up on the screen right on cue. My heart jackhammers in my chest.

'Ten minutes. I'll meet you at yours.' I reply, jumping up from my chair. Her invitation came about an hour ago, while the boys were busy having a whipping war with their ties. I could have told them, but Jazzie shut down that thought fairly quickly with a very convincing argument. Yesterday was intense. I deserve some time to decompress. I haven't had real friends before. As for the boys, they may have the illusion they own me–but no one owns me. I should be living my life the way I want to, and so on and so forth.

By the time Jazzie had finished reeling off reasons to go out and let my hair down, I'd already responded with a 'Hell yeah.' Tonight, I'm not going to be Sophia, the girl scared of her own shadow. I'm going to be Sophia, the free spirit.

Racing into the bathroom, I sigh in relief to find the window I'd pre-unlocked wasn't detected. I look to Jazzie for a quick mental check. Phone, hoodie, lack of fucks. I'm all set. Jimmying the window fully open, I twist back at the last minute to peer at the orange bottle on the dresser, one lonely pill sitting in the base. No. Not tonight, I decide before slipping out into the night air. The drainpipe, which has become my personal fireman's pole, sees me to the ground, my sneakers taking off in a run as soon as they touch the grass.

Letty's sorority house is just down the road. Music leaks from the building, the buzz of giggles almost bringing my feet to a stop. Nope, not today. I've faced enough in this past week to warrant a free pass from my anxiety. As long as my head gets the memo.

"There you are!" Letty flings the door open, a half-empty bottle of vodka in her hand. The excitement in her eyes wanes as she takes in my outfit.

"You're seriously not wearing that, are you?" I frown at my hoodie and jeans, spying the mud on my Converse.

"I mean...it's just a few girls hanging out, right?"

"Oh, you silly goose!" Letty grabs my arm and drags me inside, up her stairs, and into her bedroom. "When I said, do you want to hang with the girls tonight, I meant in the VIP section of Karlo's. Duh."

"Who's Karlo?"

"God, you're so cute. It's like having a foreign exchange student for a friend. Karlo isn't a who–it's a what. The hottest nightclub in the city, and Becca has been screwing the security guard."

"Um, lucky us," I try to not look terrified and fail. Letty tries to tug my hoodie over my head, and I quickly stop her. "Okay, okay. I'll change. Let me see what you've got." Jazzie is over my shoulder, peering into Letty's walk-in closet with me. Am I still feeling as confident about being a free spirit? Fuck no, but at least this way, I'm in charge. Slightly. My fingers brush the dresses, settling for a black long-sleeved dress with a plaid skirt attached. Small plumes of fabric emphasize the shoulders, the material thin and see through. Letty pops her head back in once I'm dressed, clumsily nudging a pair of glittery heels towards me with her foot.

"Not the most scandalous item I own, but you pull it off. The car's outside, time to go." I grab the shoes, not allowing myself to overthink. Passing the long mirror on the back of the door, I still. My pale blue hair is fluffed, scattering wildly around my shoulder. A pink twinge hints at my cheeks, complimenting my full lips. My red bra appears to be a deeper shade of crimson through the dress, and in the heels, my legs appear incredibly long. Thankful, I've been keeping up with regularly shaving now the boys seem to be lingering around me all the time.

*I would*, Jazzie bobs her brows at me. I roll my eyes, grab my phone, and rush out of Letty's house. The pick-up truck is starting to leave, a whole crowd of girls beckoning me into the back. I totter as best I can until a host of hands reach out and lift me the rest of the way. I land hard on my ass, but laughter spills from my lips. The frat and sorority houses grow smaller in the distance, and my spirit feels like it's bursting from my body, soaring high above. This is what living feels like. Tonight, I'm breaking free of the chains that bind me.

***

The pulsing bass of the nightclub hits me as soon as we step inside. Becca has hung back to make out with her security guard boyfriend, which I quickly realized was how the other six of us were to sneak through the open double doors. Not quite the welcome I had pictured.

The air is heavy with a mixture of sweat, smoke, and the overpowering scent of cheap perfume and cologne. A blur of neon lights and flashing strobes assault me, illuminating the dance floor and creating pockets of shadows where silhouettes sway to the beat. Glittering confetti rains down from the ceiling, shimmering over a chaotic frenzy of colors and movement. My fingernails dig into my palm. I take a step back, bumping into the people behind me, who proceed to shove me back into the midst of my own group.

The DJ's voice booms through the speakers, telling all of the girls who dressed to impress to get their asses on the dancefloor and show him some moves. I glance down at Letty's dress on my body. The way it moves with my every step, hugging my curves...well, I'm trying my best to feel empowered.

"Let's get a drink!" Letty shouts over the music, pulling me by the hand through the throng of people. We elbow our way to the bar as a group. I let the girls form a circle of protection around me. My chest tightens, the roar of the crowd causing tremors deep within. Once upon a time, the noise and amount of people wouldn't have even crossed my mind. I have to keep reminding myself that no one is even looking my way. I'm just another number to the body count, nothing else. I can do this. I will do this.

Taking the glass bottle Letty hands me, I swallow it down without reading the label, trying to quell the anxiety swirling inside. It burns my throat, and I hiss, half choking as she grabs my left wrist and drags me into the sea of bodies. I go into full fight-or-flight, twisting my scarred wrist from her grip with too much force.

"Relax, Sophia!" Letty exclaims, tugging me onto the dance floor. "It's all just a bit of fun!" For the briefest moment, I stand and watch Letty throw her arms in the air and dance with the biggest smile on her face. Jealously courses through me. How easy it is for some people, while the rest of us struggle just getting out of bed some days. I want to be like her more than I care to admit. Downing the drink in my hand, I put it in some stranger's hand and dive forward.

I'm beyond awkward. Off beat, always missing the moments where the music dies, and everyone knows to still, but I'm going for it. Swaying my hips, rolling my hands to and fro. When the floor is this crowded, it doesn't matter what I do—no one can see beyond their own cramped bubble anyway. Soon enough, the music becomes a balm to my frayed nerves, and impossibly, I feel something akin to peace. There's an odd sense of freedom in being surrounded by so many people yet remaining utterly anonymous.

As the night progresses, I drink more and dance harder, forgetting my earlier concerns. The bar quickly becomes a place of comfort, its vibrant shots and spirits a lifeline I quickly come to depend on. Once I become familiar and on a first-name basis with Antonio, the bartender, the rest of my inhibitions melt away. Jazzie doesn't make an appearance, her voice not loud enough to be heard. I completely tune out my own instincts, discovering the ease with which laughter bubbles from my mouth as the room starts to tilt slightly.

"Having fun?" Letty grins as she twirls me around, her giggling ringing clear above the pounding music.

"Actually, yeah," I admit, surprised at myself. Free from the constraints and expectations of the university, for once, I feel normal. Somewhere along the way, I can forget all about the Thorn Brothers. Their desires, their demands, their contract.

Hands settle on my ass, and I quickly shake them off, spinning closer to the girls I came here with. Many have paired off, finding partners for the evening. I have an undeniable sense I'm being watched, the hair on the back of my neck standing on end, but I also know I have a knack for being my own worst enemy. Nothing a trip back to Antonio can't fix.

"Back again?" he smiles, ignoring all the others bidding for his attention to lean on the bar and focus on me. "Either you have incredible stamina, or you're flattering me."

"Wouldn't option three be that I have a problem?" I raise a brow, accepting the cocktail he hands me. I'm fairly certain it was meant for someone else.

"Having a reason to keep visiting me isn't a problem at all," Antonio winks. He's a handsome enough guy, but unfortunately for him, I've been rather spoiled with good looks back on campus. Holding his gaze, I realize through my buzzed state, I'm searching for something more. I quickly decide it's the possessive edge I've come to expect. I take the drink, turning away and digging for my phone in my cleavage. There are two texts waiting for me.

**Lucas**: 'That essay had better be finished. You won't be able to string a sentence together once I get back and do everything I'm imagining to you.'

**Kyan**: 'Word of warning, Lucas won't stop talking about you. It's likely he's forgotten if anyone is having you tonight, it's me.'

I didn't expect a message from Ezra. To be fair, I didn't expect a message from any of them. Jazzie appears at a high standing table nearby, just as my self-doubt starts to settle in. I can't hear her over the music, but her lips are easy enough to read. 'Oh, they're going to be pissed.' My knees threaten to give out.

Peering back across the dance floor, I spot Letty's head bobbing amongst the rest. Slipping my drink, it doesn't seem to taste as good anymore. I wanted freedom. Or at least, I thought I did. But from the outside looking in, and from the giddiness those messages have fluttering through me, my perspective has shifted. Instead of enjoying being a nobody lost to the crowd, I frown. I'm just another number in here. Another patron for the bar, another body for strangers to grind against. Why did being the same as everyone else seem so appealing? Lucas chose me for being the direct opposite of that.

Tucking my phone away, I skate around the side of the club, making a beeline for the restrooms. That nagging feeling of being watched returns. My gaze flits from face to face, searching for any sign of the Thorn Brothers. My heart shudders. But they're not here, I tell myself. It's just my imagination, which is probably for the best because they will indeed be pissed I've snuck out and defied them. Still, now the seed of doubt has been planted, I can't seem to shake it off.

# Chapter 16

The line for the restrooms is so long, some have decided to use the hallway as an extended dancefloor. I rest against the wall, trying to settle my mind. Where my thoughts usually tumble on a never-ending loop, the alcohol only intensifies them. The ground beneath my feet doesn't feel solid, the wall shifting as I struggle to find a comfortable spot against it. A whimper escapes my lips, and I briefly wonder if I'm going to be sick.

*Should have stayed home and taken a Klonopin*, Jazzie reminds me. I couldn't agree more. As the minutes tick by and the line barely inches forward, the pressure in my bladder becomes too much to ignore.

"Damn it," I mutter under my breath. Drunk and impatient, I make a rash decision. Stumbling out of the hallway, I dodge a series of couples tucked beneath the overhang of the balcony, making out and moaning. I'm fully convinced some are having full-on sex, the musty smell of sweat stronger here than anywhere else. Between them, a slither of cool air draws me towards a side door, which promptly deposits me into an alley. I look around, my eyesight not quite quick enough to follow the spinning of my head. The alleyway is damp and stinks of stale beer, but I'm alone. Thank fuck.

Squatting behind one of the many dumpsters, I relieve myself with my head in my hands. If this isn't the initiation to becoming a fully-fledged uni student, I don't know what is. Feeling completely mortified, I shake like I have a tail and pull up my panties. Stepping out from behind the dumpster, I half-stagger towards the metal door when a group of masked men appear seemingly out of nowhere, crowding me against the cold brick wall. Ski masks cover their faces, their bodies hidden in a sea of black clothing which bleeds in our surroundings. My breath catches.

"I-I don't have anything–" I stammer, catching myself. Three figures stand stoically, cocking their heads at me with keen intensity. Motherfuckers. They move as one, grabbing my arms and pinning me against the wall. The cold seeps through the thin dress at my back, causing me to gasp. The drunken buzz makes me more responsive, the images of what they're capable of flashing before my eyes. This is perfect. Let them hunt me down, punish me in all the ways they've been promising.

A hand closes around my throat, tight enough to just about hurt. I don't resist. Dark chuckles sound from my captors, their breath clouding in front of them. The one in the center, which I decide has the same body type as Kyan, runs a finger suggestively down my chest towards my skirt. Fingers tease the hem of the fabric when a sense of resolve bursts through me.

"Wait," my brows crease. They don't stop, their grip on my wrists ironclad. Boots nudge my legs widen as a calloused hand touches my thigh. How did they even find me? Are they tracking my phone, keeping tabs?

This is my night to feel free. My chance to experience student life without them crowding me. They don't get to crash in and take control.

Rotating my wrists in a sudden flash of movement, I twist violently and manage to shake off one of the hands. Luckily, my compliance up until now has left them unprepared. I follow through with a swift elbow to the gut of the man holding my other arm. There's a grunt, a sudden exhalation of air that tells me I've hit my mark. My heart beats a wild rhythm in my chest as adrenaline floods my veins. Jazzie is cheering for me, screaming to give these boys a taste of their own medicine. They mean to scare me, but I'm not some poor defenseless girl they can manipulate. Barring stupid decisions that have brought me to this point, I've learned to take care of myself.

The grip on my other arm loosens just enough for me to slide out from between them, twisting in a way that might have been graceful if not for the lingering alcohol buzz. My heels stumble over the rough concrete, but I find my footing and bolt down the alleyway. Any semblance of control ends there.

Behind me, the stillness is shattered by curses and heavy footsteps. The world spins around me, blurring into a chaotic mess as I run blindly. I hear their footfalls growing louder. Something about the scenario becomes very real, as does the terror leaking through my chest. Every part of me screams to press on and find safety inside the club. Just a few more steps and I'll be surrounded by people, safe from their reach. But before I do, I want to drive the message home. I won't be intimidated. I won't sit around like a good little pet waiting for them to make all the decisions.

Slowing my pace slightly, I step over the threshold of the club, glancing back to see two are close behind. The idea an inebriated Jazzie whispers to me is as wild and impulsive as the wind whipping at my hair.

"Was this supposed to scare me?" I challenge them, my voice trembling only slightly. "Nice try, but you'll have to do better than that." Without warning, I strike. My heel connects with a chest, and he tumbles backward onto the damp concrete, a tangle of flailing limbs and painful grunts. Please let it be Ezra. Slamming the door closed, I drop the latch to lock the slab of metal between us. Excitement and something darker bolsters my strides towards the dance floor. It's power, I quickly realize. This is what they thrive on, and I now understand why.

Halfway towards the group of girls I came here with, my phone buzzes in my cleavage. I bark a laugh and hit the answer button.

"Oh, you must think you're so funny," I drawl into the speaker. "The masks were a real nice touch." I can't hear the response due to the music, but the name lit up on the screen shows he's listening. "How was that for a hunt, Lucas? Not as helpless as you expected." I start laughing, wandering away from the speakers. "If you'd wanted an easier prey, maybe you should have chosen someone else." My smile is so wide, it hurts. "One point to Sophia, minus fifty to Slytherin." Wait, that's not right.

"Sophia!" Lucas shouts into my ear when I can finally make out the words. "What the fuck are you talking about?!" I stop wandering around between the bodies, taking a moment to string together my thoughts.

"The...the attack you staged...in the alleyway," I reiterate.

"Attack?! What the fuck–" Lucas cries out, and another voice takes over.

"Where the fuck are you?" It's Ezra, of that I have no doubt. I shake my head. It's all part of their game to trick me, to put me on edge. And they're doing a damn good job at it.

"As if you don't know," I roll my eyes and end the call. My phone immediately vibrates in my hand, and I ignore it. They're lying. They have to be because the alternative isn't something I want to think about.

I hover, at a loss for what to do. The enjoyable buzz has flooded my system so I stop by the bar, accepting another drink and a round of flirting from Antonio. This time, I keep looking over my shoulder, waiting for the next surprise to creep up on me. This is so typical of them. I'm a fish on a hook, being given a little line, only to be reeled straight back in. But what if they're telling the truth?

I open my phone, ignoring the thirty-six missed calls, and quickly load a local tabloid site. They're supposed to be at a family event in this very city, and their parents are film stars. It shouldn't be too hard to disprove their lies. But sure enough, an article pops up beneath my thumb, added four minutes ago. "Thorn Brothers Hastily Leave Parent's Premiere.' The headline is supported by an image of the three in their perfectly fitted suits, storming toward a limousine. Pure, unadulterated anger contorts their beautiful faces. Oh, fuck.

Ice-cold dread courses through me, and I glance back at the alley door. It's no longer locked, lingering ajar with the darkness waiting just beyond. I spin around, searching the crowds. The men, I don't know who or where they are. I need to get out of here–now.

Rushing back to Letty, I grab her arm, desperation clawing at my throat. "We have to go," I plead, trying to ignore the way my vision swims. There are too many influences battling here, both internal and self-inflicted.

"Chill, Soph," Letty slurs, clearly more intoxicated than I. She's making out with a girl, their hands tangled in each other's hair as they remain pressed close. I continue to pull at her arm, begging over the beat for her to listen. Letty bats my hand away. "Loosen up and have some fun," she groans, clearly annoyed. She won't budge.

Panic builds inside me like a tidal wave; I can feel it cresting, threatening to crash down and drown me whole. Oh no, not now. This isn't the time or place to let my anxiety win. I need to escape the crowds, the suffocation.

"Where are you when I need you, Jazzie?" I whisper to myself, teeth gritted. My heart races, and my breaths come in shallow gasps as the masked men from earlier flash before my eyes. I know it's just my mind playing tricks on me, but the delusions are all too real. When Jazzie doesn't respond, I have to fake the reinforcement she normally provides. I stand still amongst the bumping bodies, closing my eyes. I've faced worse situations before. With a deep breath, I attempt to steady myself and push my fear aside.

"Fine," I mutter to myself, determination flaring in my chest. "I'll take care of myself." I make my way through the rippling bodies and pounding music, each step feeling like a battle against my senses. My pulse races as I weave past drunken dancers, their sweat-slicked skin brushing against mine.

"Stay strong, Sophia," I whisper to myself, repeating it like a mantra as I force my body to keep moving. The exit seems to recede further and further away with each step I take. The room tilts and sways as dread claws at my insides. The sea of bodies around me feels endless. They close in on me as I desperately try to navigate through the throng, making it impossible to move. To breathe. I can't blackout here. Not now.

"Focus, Sophia," I tell myself again, trying to drown out the music hammering inside my skull. I'm sure there weren't this many people earlier. I become disorientated, unable to see the way out. Hands grab me from behind. A scream rips from my throat, lost amid the pounding bass. I jerk my elbows back, aiming for the ribs of whoever has grabbed me until I'm spun around.

"Don't ever do that again," Ezra consumes my vision, his growl ripping through me. His hands are tight on my sides, but I don't care. I crumple then, crushing myself against his suit. He smells incredible, far too expensive for a club like this. Winding my arms around his waist, inside his jacket, I ground myself. Mimicking the rise and fall to his firm chest, I breathe an apology for wishing I'd kicked him on his ass. Ezra doesn't rush me, his arms a solid reminder of the dangerous situation I'd put myself in. I should have known it wasn't them. I shouldn't have let my drunken ideas bleed into reality, distorting what was with what I wanted to be. After a few minutes, he tilts my chin up, our mouths surprisingly close with the height of the heels.

"I mean it," his face doesn't show a trace of kindness. "Don't fucking do that again."

"Do what?" my voice cracks as a tear spills over. I'm a mess, breaking right before his icy, blue eyes. Ezra stands stoically, only his gaze roaming my body. Assessing for damage, I quickly decide. Amongst the strobe lights, his fine suit accentuates his dark, brooding appearance. Leaving me hanging, he twists his fingers into mine and turns away.

"Stay close," he orders. The warmth of his touch calms my racing heart ever so slightly, a mixture of relief and confusion beating within. I drop my head to the floor, feeling the softening of my resolve as we navigate through the club together. The lights cast kaleidoscopic patterns across the floor, causing me to trip over myself. Ezra's grip on my hand tightens, anchoring me in place amidst the chaos. The cold air outside physically hits me like a slap of reality. I gasp, hastily pulling to a stop.

"Wait! Th-there were men in masks," I stammer, the words spilling out in a frantic rush. "They cornered me in the alley." Ezra's jaw tightens, his eyes blazing with barely controlled fury.

"We know," he growls. "Lucas and Kyan caught sight of them doing it to another girl when we pulled up outside. They're dealing with them now." A shudder runs down my spine at the thought of those masked men, their twisted intentions clear from the predatory gleam in their eyes. And I nearly let them do it to me. I bend in half, retching. Had I not decided to play along, had I continued thinking the brothers were toying with me...Ezra lowers his jacket over my back before gathering my hair as I empty the contents of my stomach onto the sidewalk. It's not pretty, as many people passing by feel the need to comment. I wish I could disappear, just fade into nothing. When I have nothing else to bring up, I straighten as much as I dare.

"What do you mean, dealing with them?" I croak. Wiping my mouth with the back of my hand, Ezra quickly hands me an embroidered handkerchief.

"We protect what's ours," is the extent of his answer. My knees tremble as the gravity of the situation begins to hit me. Ezra's eyes are dark and stormy as swoops me up, approaching a limousine waiting at the curb. The driver opens the door, and I am surprised that Ezra doesn't just chuck me inside. Instead, the warmth of his body stays against mine, seating the pair of us behind blacked-out windows when the door is shut. At last, silence settles.

"You must think I'm such a fucking idiot," I grumble, slumping into him further. As long as Ezra isn't insisting I should get off his lap, I have no intention to. I need the comfort, the reassurance. "How did you get here so fast?"

"When we couldn't get a hold of you, we started calling around the girls you tend to have lunch with. We figured one would know where you were," he grunts, his eyes never leaving mine. His anger is palpable, a living, breathing force. It crashes against me like waves, leaving me breathless and uncertain. I knew he'd be pissed, more than the others, but this...this feels like something more.

"I-I'm sorry for sneaking out," I stammer, lowering my head in shame. My apology feels hollow, inadequate given the danger I've put myself in tonight. But it's all I have to offer in this moment. Ezra remains silent, his grip on me tightening ever so slightly as if to remind me of the consequences of my actions. For the first time since meeting him, I truly understand the power he wields over me–and the vulnerability that comes with it. That very same vulnerability I was running away from. "I just...I didn't want to get to the point of feeling trapped," I admit quietly.

"Trapped?" Ezra's voice is barely audible above the hum of the engine, but the shift of intensity in his eyes speaks volumes. "Sophia," he groans. My name on his lips, the way he says it like a curse and a prayer, has my stomach tightening in knots. "You have more liberties than you know what to do with. You're not like any of the other pets we've had. You're not trying to screw us for the fame or money. We've already broken several of our own rules for you, and now," he looks away. My diaphragm has constricted, and I can't let him leave me hanging.

"And now?"

"Now we're more invested than usual. It's making us act out. All I want to do is jump out of his car and get my own pound of flesh from the assholes who scared you. But that would mean putting you down, and I'm not quite ready for that yet." I swallow hard. The others may have been forthcoming with their possessiveness and lust, but not Ezra. I thought I was merely an inconvenience to him.

"I didn't think you cared," I admit quietly, my voice small and fragile in the darkness. It's a confession I never thought I'd make, but as Ezra's fingers gently curl around my chin, forcing me to meet his intense gaze, I can't hold back any longer. The passing headlights slice through the shadows, casting a flickering dance of light and dark across Ezra's face. For a moment, I see a hint of vulnerability in his eyes, a fleeting glimpse of the boy who hides behind the mask of the bully.

"Listen to me, Sophia," he commands softly, the rough edge in his voice betraying his own uncertainty. "We care more than you can possibly know. But you have to understand how dangerous this world can be. You're quickly becoming too important for us to lose."

His words leave me reeling, caught off guard by the underlying tenderness in his tone. I, too, can no longer deny the feelings that have been growing inside me, the tendrils of affection and desire that have slowly wrapped themselves into something unmovable.

"In the club, you told me not to do something again. What was it?" I plead with my eyes, striking while Ezra is finally opening up. His fingers withdraw from my chin, the inevitable pull of his affection closing off.

"Don't scare us like that again." Ezra's expression softens, the anger in his eyes giving way to something far more tender–and infinitely more terrifying. He doesn't say anything else, but his silence speaks louder than his words ever could. In that moment, I realize that despite my best efforts, I'm already bound to him and his brothers. And as much as the thought terrifies me, there's a part of me that can't help but crave the safety and security they offer. Ezra dips his head, his lips on the corner of my mouth. I shift my head, our noses brushing as the door across the cab flies open.

"Give her to me," Lucas throws himself into the middle seat, his expression closed. Kyan drops in a moment later, closing us inside. Ezra doesn't hesitate, tossing me into Lucas' lap as if we weren't in the midst of an intense conversation. Lucas is far more forthcoming with his thoughts and feelings.

"Fuck, Beautiful. "Are you okay?" Lucas whispers in my ear, void of his usual playfulness. "Tell me those bastards didn't hurt you. Tell me they didn't...touch you," he rasps desperately.

"I-I'm fine, Lucas," I choke out, the words tasting like ash on my tongue. In truth, I'm far from okay, but admitting defeat isn't in my nature. I'll decompress later. His hands brush my thighs, a mix of deeper shades blooming across his knuckles. I shudder. Lucas buries his face in my neck. The warmth of his breath against my skin sends shivers down my spine. No more words are exchanged as Kyan orders the driver to take us home.

Home. Safety. The concept feels foreign to me, but at this moment, I crave it more than ever before. As we drive through the city streets, the lights reflect off the limousine's windows. My head spins, the alcohol still heavy in my system, and I struggle to make sense of my conflicting emotions.

"Lucas," I whisper, my voice shaky. "What happens now?" He pulls back slightly, his green eyes searching mine.

"Being ours doesn't mean you're a prisoner. Just give us a heads-up where you're going next time, yeah?" Despite myself, I smile and duck my head. Nodding, his arms wind around my body. Kyan leans over to press a kiss to my forehead.

"Let's get you back to your dorm. I'm sure you'll want some time to-"

"No!" I jolt upright and say a little too harshly. All sets of eyes land on me, including the driver's in the rearview mirror. "I...um, can I stay at the Manor tonight? I'm pretty sure my roommate is still stealing from me." The arms around my waist tighten. It's probably the alcohol making me see things, but I'm certain the boys all shift closer. It's Ezra's approving grunt which untenses my shoulders.

"We'll protect you, Sophia. Always," he grumbles.

His words settle in my heart like a comforting blanket, and I realize that the contract sitting in my backpack back at the dorm doesn't feel like a manacle anymore. Instead, it feels like a vow of protection—one that I suddenly crave with every fiber of my being.

## Chapter 17

"Is this seat taken?" I nudge Letty, gesturing to her side. The lecture hall isn't half-filled yet, considering I'm *early*. Finally, at last, I'm awake and caffeinated enough to be early for class. Let that be an omen for the rest of today.

"Oh hey! No, not at all. Come sit," Letty moves her backpack. I settle, pulling out the foldable table from between the seats and positioning it in front of me. "I haven't seen you since Karlo's; I was starting to worry something had happened." I smile easily, not commenting on the fact that was days ago and she was only just 'starting' to worry. I could have been dead in a ditch somewhere.

Instead, I continue setting up my notepad and textbook. Everyone else present is typing on a laptop, but I prefer good old-fashioned paper and highlighters. It helps organize my mind. Letty tosses her brunette braid over her shoulder and presses me further. "Have you been sick?"

"Erm," my cheeks flush. How can I casually announce I've not left Thorn Manor for the past few days? Don't get me wrong, I've probably studied longer and harder than anyone in this room, between countless orgasms and several naps. I have to admit, it's been glorious, even if we're still on a one-at-time regime. Letty's large eyes blink, still waiting for my answer. "Not physically. I just needed a few mental health days. You know how it is." Her smile grows as she eases back into her seat.

"Oh, absolutely–you have to look after yourself first. Not everyone is comfortable taking those days when needed, so good for you." Letty smiles kindly, and I decide she's a good friend to keep around, even if she's a little air-headed.

*That's not fair*, Jazzie jumps into the seat in front of me and twists back. Her black hair shifts over the backrest, the silver highlights catching the light. *Some people haven't been through what you have. Just because she doesn't understand how your mind works, doesn't make her an airhead.*

I hold my hands up in defeat and nod, answering in my mind. *Okay, okay. You're right.* Jazzie turns around to face the front of the lecture hall, while Letty side-eyes me. I suppose out of the two of us, I'm the one who would seem a few marbles sort of a netted pouch.

"At least you're doing better than Becca," Letty quickly whispers.

"Why, what happened to Becca?" I ask, my interest piqued. Other students quickly rush down the aisles, dropping into seats as Mrs. Patrick enters the hall. Letty leans into me, covering her mouth with her fluffy pen.

"Apparently, she was kicked out of her dorm without any notice and told to find her own lodgings. She can't afford to stay nearby so she's dropped out." My jaw hits the ground. That can't be anything to do with me. Surely, it's nothing to do with me. Mrs. Patrick commands everyone's attention as my mind wanders. Again.

I need to speak to the boys. They've been more distracted lately, what with the sports rally quickly coming around. I swallow thickly. This will be the first full school event where I have to sit and pretend I'm not screwing the star players.

No matter how many times Jazzie has told me to, I've refused to ask the brothers what will happen when they decide it's time to publicly claim me. In fact, I've avoided discussing the whole 'pet' situation at all costs. If I say it, if I accept it out loud, it'll become real. It'll change the casual routine I'm settling into. Sustenance, study, sex, sleep. Complete bliss, until I need to leave the house and re-enter the real world.

Hence why I sought out Letty, figuring I'd get answers another way. I wait until Mrs. Patrick begins reading a segment of Shakespeare, letting herself get carried away, before leaning into Letty's side.

"Can I ask you something?" I whisper. Letty nods, keeping her eyes forward. "This whole Pet thing with the Thorn Brothers. I just...I don't understand why three men like them would want to share one woman. Surely there are so many girls throwing themselves at their feet?"

"It goes back to their orphanage days," Letty replies, keeping her voice low. "From what I understand, they were constantly running away, and there was a time all three would need to share a single meal or swap around who would get to wear a jacket that day. For nostalgia, I suppose, they just like to share, and this is their last chance to do so." My gut coils into a ball, my heart tugging heavily in my chest.

"What do you mean?" I look out the corner of my eye. Letty slumps lower, covering her mouth with her hand.

"I don't have all the details. Something about a prestigious family in Dubai who were seeking an arranged marriage for their daughter. They have big connections with the adoptive father and his business, so it made sense one of the Thorns would take her as his bride. Lucas is the oldest," Letty half shrugs. "He'll be wed and living in Dubai by the end of summer. Whoever they've chosen as their last pet, they'll need her to unite them more than any of the others have."

"*No pressure then,*" Jazzie chuckles from her seat, throwing up a peace sign. I scowl at the back of her head. Sometimes I don't know why my mind insists on still seeing her everywhere I go, but I couldn't be without her either. She's the leech I can't withdraw from my system, the crutch I'm too dependent on. But even she hasn't been as present while the Thorns have seen me comatosed from coming and drowning in dick.

"Miss Chambers," that familiar shrill voice comes. I drag my gaze up to find Mrs. Patrick sneering at me instead. "Would you like to indulge us in the ways Shakespeare uses environmental imagery in his work?"

"Gladly. Shakespeare used descriptions of the landscapes to convey important messages that are essential to the plot. For instance, in "A Midsummer Night's Dream," the imagery of the Moon plays a vital role in building the story and dialogs between the characters."

I raise a brow, staring down Mrs. Patrick until she gets the message to leave me alone from now on. As it turns out, Ezra grilling me has its uses. We already covered this module of the course and have started on the next. If I get top marks in his next pop quiz, Ezra has promised to eat me out like a crazed lion destroying a carcass–his words.

Mrs. Patrick stands stunned, before moving on to insult someone else's intelligence. It was rather ballsy of her to call me out after Kyan's warning, but I don't need his protection. I can handle myself just fine.

For the rest of the lesson, I force myself to concentrate. Despite my mind reeling, and my heart both heavy and light at the same time, I won't fall behind. I won't give Mrs. Patrick the satisfaction. Jotting down notes, managing to hold three highlighters between my fingers at once, the bell shocks the life out of me. It's over already? Letty is packing up and preparing to leave as I remember I had more questions. I'd rather not badger the Thorns with my curiosity, and Letty is proving to be my best source of information. Hastily grabbing my backpack, I shoot up the steps after her.

"So, the pet they chose," I nudge her shoulder, keeping my voice low. "Do they take her home to meet the family, buy her gifts and stuff like that? It's like hiring a girlfriend and buying her off with nice things?" If Letty finds my questions strange, her laugh doesn't show it.

"Oh no, nothing like that. It's literally sex on demand. Sometimes, the chosen girl can supply snacks to their buddies, be shown off at parties, sit with them at lunch. That sort of thing."

"Have they ever grown attached to one?" I frown, hanging off her every word. "Maybe held onto a girl for longer than a semester?" I follow Letty down the hallway to a lecture I don't even take. She pauses by the door, looking me over. I hide a blush, trying to appear genuinely curious. I need to know where I stand, and what the pets before me did.

"Hmmm, nope. It's more like a business agreement honestly. Everyone knows their role, and there's no place for affection." Shrugging one shoulder, Letty smiles and tells me she'll see me in the canteen later. I wave her off, walking a few paces backward. Just a business agreement, no affection. It doesn't seem to sit right with what I've expected so far. My phone pings, alerting me I have a counseling session in five minutes with Lorna. For the first time, I don't drag my feet, ready and smiling as Lorna opens her door.

"Sophia! How lovely to see you. Please come in." I step over the threshold of her office, a skip in my step. Tonight, as a reward for attending my counseling session, Kyan is setting up a movie night in the lounge. I don't care what we're watching. All I know is there will be tons of affection, and Lucas is serving the snacks, having offered to be my butler in the buff. Now I know that's not something a typical Pet would experience, I'm even more excited.

## Chapter 18

The sun is especially warm today, a subtle breeze shifting through my hair. There's never been a better time to have a free period. I should spend this afternoon studying some more, but the call of a grassy bank and a book was too much to deny. Sitting on my jacket, I tug up my sleeves marginally. Just enough to expose some wrist. My legs are bare in a pair of khaki shorts, bathed with heat as I recline fully onto my back.

"Hey there, you sexy minx." Lucas' shadow is cast over my face. Peering at him through my glasses, I suddenly bolt upright, checking no one else is nearby.

"What are you doing here?" I hug my book to my chest like armor, as if Lucas would dive on top of me if I didn't.

"Looking for you, obviously. I thought you'd be back at ours after lunch."

"Um...no?" I frown. Racking my brain, I don't think I've missed a memo. Granted, I have been heading back to theirs most days, favoring to be around people rather than sit alone in my dorm. Even the basketball team being noisy in the kitchen or shouting at their video games doesn't bother me. They're apparently well-trained enough to not pay me any attention, which I prefer. "Were you guys waiting for me?"

"Not particularly," Lucas smirks and sits at my side. Hanging his arms over his knees, he looks across the campus to where the library's spires can be seen. "I just figured you'd want to get ready for the gallery fundraiser tonight. Maybe I'm presuming too much, but I figured you might need one of these." Reaching into his jacket pocket, Lucas pulls out a single blue pill. My eyebrows hit my hairline.

"You hate me taking meds," I watch the side of his face carefully. Lucas keeps his smirk in place, despite the sigh that steady moves from his chest to his nose.

"I'm not a doctor or a psychiatrist, as Kyan keeps telling me." Lucas looks at me with a playful glint in his green eyes. "I don't *hate* you taking what you need. My only hope is that if we can help build your confidence, if we show you how strong you can be, you might not have to rely on them as much. A life of synthetic highs...it's not what I want for you." His smile slips the smallest bit as he places the pill on my palm. I remember back to what Ezra said in the hospital, about his mom overdosing. I chew on the inside of my cheek.

"And why would I need to relax for an art show?"

"The gallery fundraiser," Lucas corrects. He drops back to lean on his elbows. "Don't you read the student messages and billboards? The school is putting on a gala to raise money for abandoned and abused children, and all of our families are invited." I shoot to my feet, the book falling aside. Families? Parents?

"But, surely they...they have to be invited, right? I would have to send a personal invite if...if..." I twist back to Lucas, no longer caring if anyone is nearby. He looks at me too apologetically, and my heart stalls.

"I mean, unless they read the university newsletters, which are sent out electronically." My eyes widen, the world around me tilting. Before I collapse, or utterly lose my shit, I throw the blue pill into my mouth and swallow it dry. Nothing happens at first, the tremors in my limbs taking over. My mother wouldn't come here. She won't come, right? I look to Jazzie leaning against a nearby tree.

*Depends,* she half-shrugs. *How vindictive do you think mommy is feeling today?* Oh god, she's totally coming. I wrap a hand around my throat, focusing on the rise and fall of my chest.

"Come on, let's get you back." Lucas wraps an arm around my shoulders. He carries my backpack and the library book, leading me down the grassy bank.

A feeling of persistent dread simmers, but I manage to gain some control over my breathing and stammer out a weak, "Okay." My limbs feel leaden, but Lucas is patient, matching his stride with mine. The chill of fear lingers, but the Klonopin starts to work, the edges of my anxiety beginning to blur and fade.

The walk back to Thorn Manor is quiet, framed by the gentle squelch of grass under our feet and a distant grind of traffic. The breeze continues to play with my hair, and I use it as a focus point, trying to enjoy the remainder of the afternoon rather than let myself spiral. For an introvert to choose to be outside, it must have been a glorious afternoon. I just can't summon the energy to enjoy it now.

As we near the huge whitewashed buildings, I catch sight of Kyan waiting on the porch. He spots us and moves toward us with a worried frown on his face. Striding to a stop in front of me on the stone path, he hesitates, fisting his hands to hold back from taking my face and kissing me. Despite everything we've been through and the amount of public interactions we've had, they're still honoring my request to keep us a secret. I think it adds to the appeal.

"They're here," Kyan murmurs towards Lucas, his fathomless dark eyes continually returning to me. My stomach drops.

"Who's here?" I ask as a woman's laugh comes from inside. Both boys slip their hands into mine, interlocking my fingers. I wonder if they knew I was about to bolt. Guiding me towards the house, the sound of glasses clinking tickles out of the open door.

"Ahh, there you are!" A couple beam as we step into the dining room. They're currently mid-conversation with Ezra, who is more animated than I've ever seen. Holding out his arms, the suited male pats Lucas hard on the back. "Ezra was just telling me about the sport's rally this weekend. I hope you've doubled your drills."

"Yes, sir," Lucas chuckles. "Five every morning and extra after lunch, as Coach recommended." While the men catch up, my gaze drifts. The woman is incredibly beautiful, her long blonde hair flowing behind her like the train of her turquoise dress.

"You must be Sophia! I've heard so much about you," she draws me in for a tight hug. Over her shoulder, I watch Lucas still embraced by the man, his gray peppered hair the only hint he's slightly older. Straight teeth shine from his full-bodied smile, a distinct lack of wrinkles around his bold, blue eyes. He turns to me after I've been released, his handshake crushing.

"Sophia, these are our parents," Lucas begins introductions. My stomach is churning as Isabella and Mason Taylor look me over, not showing their scrutiny of my baggy sweatshirt and short shorts. From the walk, mud cakes my Converse, and my hair is a knotted mess. Still, they don't reel back in disgust as I'd expected.

"It's so good to finally meet the girl who's got our boys tripping over themselves," Mason chuckles. Isabella pats his bicep.

"You must be very special, my dear." Her eyes twinkle, a similar hint of mischief in them as I've seen in Lucas. I blush, trying to hide behind my hair. Ezra appears then, standing between his adoptive parents and folding his large arms.

"You're embarrassing the poor girl," he rolls his blue eyes. "Go get showered and dressed. There's a surprise waiting for you in your room," Ezra jerks his head, effectively dismissing me.

Whether he intended to give me a moment of reprieve or was just being an asshole, I'm thankful for the escape. I run up to the bedroom I've been designated, stopping short when I find all of my bags at the foot of the bed. The rest of my belongings have been packed up into boxes and placed beneath the window. Shit, it's true. I caused Becca to get kicked out of school.

*I mean, technically, her thieving got her kicked out.* Jazzie sits on the dresser and swings her legs. I turn my back, unable to deal with this right now.

My thought process is slow, my eyes gliding over how much care has been taken to bubble wrap my photo frame and pencil pot. I glance at the bathroom, then back to the bed. I'm not prepared for this, the possibility of seeing my mother. We've met twice since I was released from juvie, and in both instances, I came away more determined than ever to not turn out like her.

My feet move of their own accord, and before I know it, I've kicked off my sneakers, shed my clothes down to my underwear, and crawled beneath the duvet. My hands claw the covers tighter into my body, whereas I puff up the space around my head like an air bubble. Something I've perfected to suit me in times of need. Enough space to breathe, yet tucked in nice and secure while my heart thunders out of sync.

"Stupid, stupid, stupid." I rock slightly, huffing to myself. "Why do I have to be so stupid?" A weight settles on the side of the mattress, so gradually, I trick myself into thinking it's Jazzie. The cover around my head is slowly peeled back, and without looking at me, Kyan strokes my hair.

"How did I know I'd find you like this?" His voice is low. I wriggle forward, curling myself around his back and resting my head on his lap.

"I don't want you to meet her," I shudder. Kyan's fingers are still in my hair, gently working the knots out and smoothing his palm over my head.

"Your mom?" He enquiries after a minute of silence. I nod against his thigh. A deep exhale leaves Kyan before he shifts, lowering himself onto the floor. His head lays on the mattress next to mine, those black eyes boring into mine. "You won't find others who understand our parents don't define us like we do." I wince, remembering the power couple downstairs adopted Kyan and his brothers for a reason.

"I'm sorry," I whisper. "I didn't think–" Kyan quickly hushes me, his fingers stroking my jaw.

"Our pasts are just that. Memories we learn to live with. If today will prove too painful, then we'll stay right here. We can hide away until morning." I smile then, leaning forward. Kyan takes the hint and kisses me, slowly, thoroughly. He captivates my lips with a surprising softness. His tongue teases the tip of mine but doesn't push beyond that. When Kyan pulls back, tears are lingering in my lashes. If I was worried about falling for him before, that offer, that level of understanding, just cemented it.

"No, we'll go," I nod in an attempt to convince both of us. Kyan watches me carefully, ready to argue, but I pull myself upright. The cover falls to my waist as I move my legs to sit either side of his wide shoulders. Both of our eyes drop to the scar on my arm at the same time. My chest stills, mid-breath. Kyan flicks his gaze to me, a small pull between his brows asking me to trust him. Fingers wrap around my wrist, tenderly turning my arm over so the scar is faced upward. Then, his head is lowering. Those full, gentle lips press to the raised blemish marring my skin. I try to look away, but Kyan won't let me. Cupping my jaw, he kneels up to meet my gaze.

"Nothing about you, or your past, will stop me from wanting you." I swallow hard, hearing voices growing closer to the door. Reaching for my sweatshirt, I hug it to my chest, concealing my arm inside. Our reprieve is up, and it's time to pull my big-girl panties on. Not literally, Lucas would never allow it.

"Are we ready yet?" the man in question pops his head around the door. Ezra just kicks it wide open. Both of their brows raise at finding me in bed with Kyan's head in the apex of my thighs. I push myself up on his shoulders, clearing my throat.

"Kyan was just advising me on what to wear," I search for an excuse. Lucas chuckles, stepping inside as Ezra closes the door behind him.

"Yeah, right. If that's the case, you'd better get naked, Pretty Girl. Apparently, there's a lesson that needs to be taught about sneaking off without inviting the rest of us, and we've got about..." Lucas looks at his Rolex. "Eleven minutes to teach it."

## Chapter 19

Passing beneath a balloon arch of rose golds and pale pinks, we step into the converted great hall. Sashes in similar colors have been draped across the walls, beneath high, narrow windows. The atmosphere is alive, a sea of smiling faces and humorous mutterings sounding around the artwork on show. My heart flutters in my chest, but this is fine. Nothing like the unease I had entering the nightclub. This is local and safe, not to mention I have a set of bodyguards glued to my back and sides.

I text ahead to check if Letty and the other girls would be attending tonight. Apparently, they swung by earlier before heading to a live poetry reading upstate. I declined the invitation to join, as much as I'd like to escape the possibility of seeing my mom. Some demons we have to face, and I'd rather do it with the Thorns nearby.

"Welcome." We're greeted by a young woman in the same white shirt, black slacks, and braces as the rest of the waiting staff. She pauses long enough for each of us to take a flute of champagne from her tray, then hands me a program from the apron tied at her waist. I flick through the pages, sipping the bubbly liquid. It pools within my belly, combatting the nervous edge I'm forcing myself to keep in check. It's a good distraction while the boys lead me and their parents towards the first painting in the pop-up exhibition.

The art students present are dressed to impress, their suits and gowns a touch more extravagant than expected. Following the Thorns' advice, I've donned a burgundy leather skirt, a black scalloped vest, and small heels. Kyan had slipped his jacket over my shoulders, allowing me to hide my scarred arm from view. Something he made sure to tell me was only for my comfort.

The boys opted for smart shirts, rolled up to the elbows, collars popped, and dark jeans. Their muscles are deliciously pressing against the shirt fabric, each flex of their shoulders rippling enough to make me bite down on my bottom lip.

Isabella and Mason admire the art pieces, from the smallest painting with painstaking detail to the biggest sculpture of a sunflower. No matter their celebrity status—which doesn't go unnoticed by the school paper's photographer—they make sure to stop and talk with every artist. I'm a step behind, listening intently to the questions and answers. Art isn't a talent I've been blessed with, but I've often wondered how different life could have been if I had such an outlet. A way to turn my anxiety into craft and in turn, rid it from my system.

*I don't think we've done too badly,* Jazzie scoffs in my ears. Batting her away with a swish of my hair, I lock myself back into the conversation Isabella is having with an eccentric artist. Her gaze is appreciative and curious of both him and his artwork. His hair is half green, half purple, split directly down the center and his face holds multiple piercings. He smiles wide through the gap in his front teeth and talks animatedly about his clay model.

"It's a true representation of the fight for freedom against those who refuse to question the conceptualism of normality," he beams. Isabella seems to be hanging off his every word, while Mason and his boys have to walk away to hide their sniggers. I raise a brow at the sculpture. It's a giant cock, the length and girth of my arm, trapped within a cage of barbed wire. The longer I look, the more I can appreciate how the spokes appear to be pushing into the flesh with realistic indents. It's the bead of precum seeping from the end I'm not sure about.

"Wow, thank you, my dear," Isabella shakes his hand for the second time. Winding her arm in mine, unknowingly brushing over my scar, she guides me away whilst beckoning a second glass of champagne from the waiter. "What a load of bollocks," she mutters into my ear as I take a sip. I spray my drink, choking slightly. "If you're into torture play, just say that." My eyes widen while Isabella's sparkle. She winks at me, and we move on. We stop at the next piece, an installation made from recycled plastic bottles.

"What do you think of this one, Sophia?" the actress waves her hand to the turtle's outline. I study the piece, but my thoughts are elsewhere, my eyes darting around the room, searching for any sign of my mother.

"It's nice," I reply absentmindedly, barely registering the bold colors and intricate details weaved into the plastic. The boys have fully abandoned us now, but I can still hear their laughter from across the hall. Fuck knows what they've found now.

"By the way, I wanted to tell you how glad I am that the boys have chosen you as their pet," Isabella says casually as if discussing the weather. I still, eyes widening as I stare at her.

"You know about that?" My throat goes dry.

"Of course," she laughs, her eyes crinkling with warmth. "The boys are very open with us about their antics. For years after we'd adopted them as children, we attended family therapy twice a week. Communication is key in forming a trusting foundation." She nods knowingly.

"And it does bother you? That they, you know, share one lover for a semester at a time?" I keep my voice low, not wanting to attract attention. We don't interact with the art students often, since their studios are on the far side of the campus and we work on opposite timetables, but they will still be very aware of the Pet Internship Program. Isabella shifts to wind her arm around my shoulders, saving me further discomfort by speaking into my ear.

"If you'd seen them the way I had, you'd understand. Not every relationship needs to be conventional to make sense." She glances over, spotting the boys and their father snickering at some private joke. The love between them is palpable, and I can't help but feel a pang of envy.

"We welcomed them into a mansion, and gave them lives they could have only dreamed of. But every night, we'd hear the scuffing of feet down the hall, and each morning found them sharing one bed. It got to the point where one refused any special treatment without the others receiving it, even on their own birthdays. To be quite honest with you, I'd started to worry I'd have a very different legal problem on my hands. The internship they've created, it's another way of keeping them connected."

Isabella breathes a sigh of relief as my mind trips over itself. A different legal problem–as in, her adoptive sons forming a sexual relationship with each other? I can't even imagine what kind of implications that would have on their celebrity status.

"Is that why–" I blurt, catching myself. Isabella's gaze shifts to mine, and she nods for me to speak freely. "Is that why you're marrying Lucas off after graduation?" My cheeks burn, but I need to know. If Isabella and Mason are so understanding of their sons' need to be connected, why would they try to sever it so harshly? Isabella's smile takes on a sad edge.

"We've only ever wanted what's best for our boys," she says softly. We arrive at the next painting, a gigantic canvas of erupting color. Each vibrant stroke is chaotic, smeared layers from a palette knife creating a tacky texture against the smooth background. I forget to blink.

"Wow."

"You like this one?" Isabella watches me quizzically. The artist is a short girl, barely five feet. She watches me, too, drinking in my response to her piece. The smudge of purple on her cheek would suggest she was working on it right up until the show began. I can sense that in the painting; how she gave herself to the paint and, in turn, has given me a spectacle to lose myself in. I remember to nod at Isabella's question.

"This one is my favorite by far. I imagine...It's what the inside of my brain looks like." Snapping out of my spell, I realize I just said that out loud. My cheeks heat instantly, and I try to retract myself from the arm Isabella has loosely draped around my back. Fuck, she must think I'm a nutcase. But instead of concern, her eyes meet mine, and she smiles warmly, embracing me with understanding.

"My boys are lucky to have you, Sophia." Before I can respond, the doors to the canteen are announced as open, and the crowd begins to move toward them. Isabella and I join the flow of people, but my newfound sense of comfort is short-lived.

"Sophia!" a voice calls out, and my heart sinks. Even before I see her face, all the anxiety I'd been suppressing comes flooding back. Not now. Not ever again. My mom elbows her way through the crowd and wraps her arms around me in a rough hug, one that feels more invasive than affectionate. My body stiffens, but I force myself to endure it for the sake of those looking on.

"Mom," I mutter, keeping my eyes glued to the floor. It's impossible to avoid any further introductions as the boys zero in on me in full defense mode. Quickly reeling off names, I try to walk on, glazing over the fact a pair of celebrities are shaking my mom's hand. The boys remain with me, forcing her to run around them to regain my attention.

"My, my," her blue eyes twinkle. They're the same shade as mine, but I'm still unnerved when they are anything but dazed from whatever drug she's currently on. Keeping her voice quiet, she tries to hide beneath the soft music and chatter around us. "Someone's landed on her feet. I told you years ago you'd have the perfect body for whoring yourself out." She flicks my scalloped bra cup and bobs her brows. I hear a growl behind me, but Lucas stops Ezra from acting out. When it comes to my mother, the insults don't quite hit the same. As if I'm numb to her opinions.

"Jude sure seemed to think I was whore material," I comment back in a low, deadly tone. My mom inhales sharply but continues walking at my side.

She has always defended her drug dealer boyfriend, stating that he would never creep up to my safe space in the attic and try to molest me. Not that she would have known, being passed out on the sofa, but that's not the story she gave the jury. She told them the pair were enjoying a movie together when I attacked him with a kitchen knife, scarring his face for life. A brutal reminder that this girl knew his type and snuck the weapon out every time he visited. Defending myself cost me two years of my life in a juvenile detention center, and if it hadn't been for the failed drug tests of the defendant, it would have likely been more.

I will my lungs to expand with air and focus on putting one foot in front of the other. Anyone else would refuse to ever see or talk to their mom again, but I've fallen for the 'I've changed, I'm sober now' excuse before. Maybe because I want the hope that it's achievable, that there's a chance I'll kick my own addiction one day. Now I'm twenty-four, my confidence in myself is waning.

Stepping into the canteen, I barely recognize the place we destroyed with spaghetti a few weeks ago. Void of the long tables and benches, it's been transformed into an elegant dining area. Small tables for six are dressed with white tablecloths and a numbered paddle has been placed on individual placemats. The color scheme for the chairs matches the great hall, rose gold bows wrapped around the chairs, and pale pink confetti sprinkled over the floor. A podium sits in front of the shutters, which have been covered with a huge auction poster.

Lucas ushers me to a table with the rest of the Thorns, his hand on the small of my back, providing a comforting presence as curious eyes follow us. I shrug them off, grateful for Letty's absence. This night is already complicated enough without adding her judgment to the mix. My mother is forced to sit alone at the adjoining table, although she scrapes her chair closer to me.

"Good evening, all," a man steps onto the podium, his warm smile curving around the microphone. He's tall and slender, his fine suit rivaling Mason's. "I'm Dean O'Sullivan, and it's with great pleasure that I welcome you all to our charity fundraiser. We are extremely fortunate to have such talented young artists in our midst, who have been eager to give back to the community. Let's give them all a hand, shall we?" A long line of art students walk into the canteen, waving as we applaud. Once everyone has squeezed in, Dean O'Sullivan moves on to introduce the head of the art department, Ms. Carver, to get the main event underway.

I settle back, Kyan's arm across my chair. His dark eyes sweep over me regularly, a note of concern held within. All three brothers are as close as can be, and across the table, Isabella checks I'm okay without a sound passing her lips. I nod, smiling genuinely. It's much easier knowing they're aware of the 'pet' agreement, so it doesn't seem like I'm some random slut who's taking advantage. Not to them, at least. My mother watches every movement like a hawk.

One at a time, Ms. Carver introduces all the art students on the program. They hold up a large image of their piece, beaming with pride. You can tell which table belongs to which student by the rambunctious cheering, and parents standing to capture photos on their smartphones. My nose tingles with the sensation that I might tear up, but I push it down. Pride is an emotion I struggle with.

At our table, hidden in the back, we clap and listen to the bidding in mostly comfortable silence. My mom snorts and makes rude comments about the art pieces, causing my cheeks to burn with embarrassment. I clench my fists under the table, trying to ignore her behavior and focus on the auction instead.

When the abstract painting is announced, I sit up a little straighter. The image on the tiny woman's board doesn't do it justice. If we hadn't stopped to appreciate it in person, I'd have never been able to tell how the paint is built up with layers, how the back-and-forth swirling of bold color gives my eyes a trail to follow. There isn't one focal point, unlike the printed image currently being held up on the board. The bids start low without any takers, and even Ms. Carver frowns. "That's a bid of fifty dollars, going once, going twice..." Her makeshift hammer hovers in the air. My heart drops.

"Thirty thousand dollars!" Isabella cries, her paddle flying into the air. I flinch, my jaw dropping. The canteen beats a moment of silence before Ms. Carver stutters over herself before announcing, "Sold!" The applause is deafening. The other artists pull the awestruck woman in for hugs, patting her shoulders until she believes it to be real. Placing down her board, she rushes through the tables to give Isabella a ticket stub with the number of her painting on it.

"Thank you so much!" she says, on the verge of tears. Isabella slides out a graceful hand.

"Hard work deserves to be recognized. Thank you for your contribution this evening."

My mom snorts. "Show off."

Isabella pretends not to hear her, waiting for the artist to skip away before sliding the ticket stub across the table to me.

"For you, my dear." My jaw drops, and I try to object, but Mason pulls Isabella under his arm, his eyes twinkling.

"We insist," he smiles warmly.

"But..but I don't have anywhere to put it," I blush, remembering that I'm essentially lodging at Thorn Manor. A temporary stay until the end of the semester.

"Well, then we will keep it safe for you. This will give you a reason to visit our home sometime, until you're ready to take it." Isabella smiles and I could weep right then and there. It's not the painting or the monetary value, but the thoughtfulness. Isabella knows what it meant to me. Somehow, even beyond the end of the school year, I've become welcomed in the Thorn's family home. A place I know would be filled with love and support, until a sudden bucket of ice doses the warmth that was building inside. Lucas won't be there.

As the night comes to an end, I reluctantly pull myself away from their comforting presence. They're too accepting, too easy to become wrapped up in. We stroll out of the canteen and through the central courtyard, which has come to life beneath reams of twinkling lights and ribbons. The moon is visible through a sheet of thin clouds, steadily flowing over a calm evening. I hug Isabella and Mason tightly, thanking them for a lovely evening. Pulling back from our embrace, Isabella's eyes roam over my face.

"We'll see you soon," she promises. I watch the pair walk away, hand in hand, laughing softly about something Mason whispered into his wife's ear. It all seems so simple, to be in love and to be loved in return. Something, I realize, I'm yearning for. Love and simplicity. Somehow, I know the familiar voice calling out behind me won't let that happen.

"Sophia," my mom's voice makes my heart skin, but I lift my chin, not wanting to show weakness.

"What are you even doing here, Mom?" I ask, raising a brow. Lucas dips his head to my ear.

"We'll wait just over here," he breathes. I vaguely watch out of the corner of my eye as he and Kyan have to manhandle Ezra over to the fountain, giving my mom and I some space. In the low lighting, I face her head on the first time. She's pale, the shadows under her eyes appearing too dark. Beneath her turtle-neck sweater and jeans, she's painfully thin. The only similarities we bear are the paleness of our blue eyes and the scars I know we have hidden beneath our sleeves. Although hers are entirely self-inflicted.

She swallows hard, glancing nervously at the boys before attempting to usher me further away from their protective presence. I stand my ground, not willing to let her control me any longer.

"I wanted to see my daughter," my mom tries to sound convincing. I fold my arms. "Well, I mean, that…and I've been having a rough time lately. Jude left me, and I can't cover the rent," she admits hesitantly, her eyes flickering over my shoulder to look at the boys.

"Jude left you?" I narrow my eyes. "After everything you've done to protect him?" My mom nods, a theatrical show of sniffling and tears sipping happening.

"He...he said I didn't have what he needs anymore. That I'm–I'm too old for him now." My stomach churns.

"Mom, that's sick. You know what he needed from you, right?" She looks at me too acutely. Yeah, she knew exactly why Jude had been hanging around for all these years. He was waiting for me to fail and return home. I think I'm going to be sick.

"But it's over now, and I need some help getting back on my feet. I see that...that you've made some good connections," her eyes flick back towards the boys. A stream of laughter bubbles from my mouth.

"You've got to be fucking kidding me," I sigh and turn away. My eyes met Lucas', and I nod, ready to leave. My mom rushes up behind me, grabbing my scarred arm. I jolt, shaking her off violently. Raising my arm to my chest protectively, I don't hear Kyan move before he's at my back, slipping his hand into my sleeve. He caresses my scar softly, a battle of emotions clogging in my throat. I don't shrug him off, preferring to use him as a barricade between my mom and I. The other two step into my sides.

"No, I wasn't, it's not money that I want," she insists, holding her hands up and keeping her voice low. "But I'm...I wondered when you last had your clozapine topped up. I'm struggling to stay focused. I just need a little something to help me through the day, you know? If you can spare your poor mom a handful."

I reel back as if I've been slapped. All of these weeks I've been struggling with the bare minimum, forced to struggle against my instincts to beg for a pill when life gets too hard. And now I understand, clearer than ever, why Lucas has refrained. I'm staring at the very real possibility of who I'd have become if it wasn't for him. My blood boils as I think, I'll give her a handful, alright. Lifting my free hand, Lucas catches my wrist, stilling my open palm.

"Sophia doesn't rely on that shit anymore," he states firmly. A cruel smile grows on my mom's face.

"I don't think so somehow. Sophia has an addictive personality. It's genetic." She turns her cold eyes to me, not a trace of fake tears left. "I know you have some, or at least something stronger. You don't think I see what you're doing, hanging out with these rich people? You've got connections now. It's only fair you help me out too. It's the least you could do for the inconvenience you've caused me these past few years."

My lungs constrict, and I sputter. "The inconvenience I've caused?!" my voice is low, my breathing harsh. Maybe a few years ago, I'd have lacked the self-esteem to argue, but not now. I need to cut these ties, or I'll always be dragged down by her. Standing straight, my shoulders push Kyan a step back. I can't let myself be crowded anymore. I need to stand up for myself.

"You heard Lucas. I don't take pills anymore. And for the record, you weren't wanted here. I don't want to see you ever again. Whatever happens, whether you're dying in a ditch or somehow find sobriety, I don't want to know. I'm not your daughter anymore. Jude made sure of that."

The words hang heavy in the air as I turn away from my mother, seeking solace in the men surrounding me. Their hands seek me out as if they can't hold themselves back any longer. As we walk away, leaving my mom stuttering and cursing behind, each step feels lighter. No longer will she bring me down or taint my mind with ideas that I can't be better. That I can't break free from the shadows of the past and be who I want to be.

We walk under the silvery glow of the moon, the darkness around us punctuated by the occasional streetlight. As the familiar outline of Thorn Manor comes into view, I can't help but marvel at how far I've come. Once a prisoner of my own mind, trapped in the throes of addiction and self-doubt, I've found solace and strength in the most unlikely of places—with three boys who see beyond my flaws and scars.

Ignoring the others holding my hands, Kyan's arms snake their way around my shoulders as we climb the porch steps.

"Are you okay?" he murmurs into my hair, his concern evident in his voice. I nod, feeling the weight of their support—a stark difference from the hollow emptiness that used to fill my days.

"I'll be fine in the morning," I sigh, suddenly tired. Ezra pulls me to a stop at the top step, his chest rumbling and his eyes glacial.

"Do I want to know what this Jude did, or will it land me in jail?" I smile but shake my head. This is my fight to bear, and today is the closest I've ever felt to winning it.

"They've taken enough from me already. I won't let them take you too." My words hang in the air. Glancing up, I see understanding reflected in all of their curious eyes, and I hope they feel the depth of my sincerity.

"Well, at least we have our parent's approval in choosing you," Lucas says softly, cupping my cheek. I bite back a smile.

"I'm sure they liked all your other pets just the same." Lucas brushes his thumb over my lips and shrugs.

"Wouldn't know. You're the only one they've ever met." My smile drops. Kyan presses his chest into my back.

"And just to throw it out there—our mother wasn't meant to be bidding in the auction tonight, considering it was for her charity." I close my eyes and have to focus on standing. My feet are throbbing in these heels, but it's my head that wobbles. Isabella's charity for abandoned and abused children, how could I have been so dense? Is that what she saw in me, a child who needed rescuing?

"Stop thinking, Feisty One," Lucas tips my head up, his hand skating across my neck. "You're going to give us all a headache at this rate." His hand leaves me then, but only long enough to unlock the front door and urge me to follow. Inside, the house is quiet and peaceful; no sign of the basketball team who use this place as a crash pad. No, tonight, it's a refuge from the outside world. The muted colors of the living room invite me to sink into the plush couch and exhale the tension that's been building all night.

The boys settle around me, Ezra drawing my legs onto his lap. My head is in Kyan's, and Lucas takes the floor, lowering his head on my ribs. Their presence is an anchor as I let my thoughts wander. Memories of the past—the anxiety, the hallucinations, the crushing weight of pills—threaten to resurface, but I push them away. I've fought too hard and come too far to be dragged back into that darkness.

"Thank you," I whisper, my voice barely audible above the gentle hum of the air conditioner. "For everything."

Ezra's reaction is almost imperceptible; a slight tilt of his head in my direction, but I feel the warmth of his smile rather than see it.

"We're here for you, Sophia. No matter what."

## Chapter 20

I stir the next morning with my front pressed against the warmth of a solid back. My lips press kisses against the shoulder blade beneath my face, marveling at the sweet soreness between my legs and utter lack of headache. A rumbling moan sounds, a mop of dark hair against the pillow. Ezra. Surprisingly, he's remained close all through the night, even when I came to Lucas' tongue running along the length of my slit. I thought I dreamt the way he sucked and hounded my clit, and the amount of fingers which were inside me, but I can tell now it was very much real.

Slipping out from beneath the sheets, I dress in someone's discarded t-shirt and sweatpants, following the scent of sweet baking towards the kitchen. Pancakes with syrup perhaps? I realize halfway down the stairs that my arms are uncovered, and I miss a step. Jazzie is smirking at me from the bottom as I right myself.

*Starting to feel a bit too comfortable, aren't we?* She laughs. I narrow my eyes at her and continue passed, trying not to think about it. In fact, all thoughts are erased from my mind when I turn the corner to find Kyan and Lucas wearing nothing but boxers and aprons, mixing bowls in their arms.

"What...the hell is happening in here?" I wander in. Lucas is looking over at Kyan's bowl, their hands spinning at unconceivable rates as they whip up egg whites. A timer rings and Kyan whoops, showing off his bowl as if he's won a prize.

"Stiff peaks, baby!" he laughs. Lucas keeps mixing his until they look the same.

"Alright, alright, I'll admit you won that one. Only because your wrist is stronger from jacking yourself off all the time."

"Lucas, my love. I've told you, you can jack me off whenever you like." Kyan smirks. My cheeks flush as I'm met with that mental image. The pair look over the kitchen island as if noticing me for the first time. "Oh, morning! How did you sleep?" Kyan's dark eyes are full of mischief. Just how many fingers were in me last night?

"Blissfully," I settle onto a bar stool. "Although my dreams were pretty bland. I can't even remember them, to be honest." Lucas plants his bowl down heavily and leans over the counter.

"We'll have to try twice as hard tonight then." I look away from his green gaze to hide my smirk.

"What exactly are we doing in here at..." I search for a clock. Fuck. "Ten thirty in the morning?! I'm late for class." A pair of heavy hands settle on my shoulders, forcing me to stay on my stool.

"Mrs. Patrick is sick. Your morning lecture was canceled," Ezra's voice is thick with sleep. He sits on the stool next to me, pressing his thigh against mine.

"How do you know that?"

"It was emailed to you last night," he grunts and looks over the kitchen. That's still not a complete answer. "Is all of this really necessary?" Ezra's brow raises. He's leaning his elbow on the counter, his bare chest rising and falling deeply. A smattering of dark curls curve over his pecs, dipping into his sternum. His abs twist as I follow that hairline down to his stomach and into his waistband, where his morning glory tents his shorts. I lick my lips on instinct, pulling my attention to the room when it grows silent. All three sets of predatory, hungry eyes are on me.

"Yes," Lucas forces out from his locked jaw. "It's necessary." In a flash, he pushes himself off the counter and returns to shifting flour. His easy smirk is back momentarily. "We're heading out today, Beautiful. I felt the need to put some distance between us and–" he waves his floury hand around, demonstrating the entire house and uni. I chew on my bottom lip, frowning at the mess of ingredients lining the kitchen.

"So, we're going for a picnic," Kyan supplies the rest while Ezra grumbles.

"I hate picnics. We're not a bunch of prissy little girls playing tea parties with our dolls."

I giggle at the thought of these three in frilly dresses. Kyan smirks too.

"I mean...I have a pretty little doll I'd like to play with," he winks at me. Lucas slaps his chest with a silicone spatula.

"Put your dick on hold," he rolls his eyes and turns to point the spatula at Ezra. "We know you hate picnics, which is why we–" he slaps Kyan again, dirtying his apron further, "got up at the buttfuck of dawn to make those little Eton Mess bites you like." Ezra purses his lips and sighs, muttering a quick explanation for me.

"We went to this castle ball in England once, and they had these little bowls called Eton Mess bites being served. It's a mix of meringue, berries, and cream. Anyways, I was so bored being introduced to all these socialites, that I snuck a tray into an office and hid under a desk to eat them all. Now, whenever Lucas and Kyan want to bribe me into something I don't want to do, they make them."

"It never fails, even after all these years," Kyan chuckles. I join in with their smiles, softly stroking Ezra's arm as it rests on my thigh. The energy is different this morning, infectious. As if we've broken through a wall and I'm finally getting to know what their dynamic is really like. As if they're letting me witness a side of them no one else gets to see, not even previous pets.

This time when Lucas spins his dripping spatula around and tries to whack Kyan with it, Kyan's quick to grab the handle and slap it back in Lucas' face. Cream splatters across his cheek and I burst out laughing, holding my sides.

"Oh, you think that's funny, do you?" I hear Lucas rather than see him through my hysterical tears. Ezra's grip on my thigh tightens as he quickly urges me to run. A flash of auburn hair appears around this side of the counter, and I bolt, racing through the manor with a smile stretched across my face. My feet slap loudly against the marble as I skid, not knowing which way to go. My hesitation costs me greatly. Lucas' arms wind around my waist, lifting me from the ground as he smears a handful of cream all over my face and hair. Damn, that boy loves a chase.

"You guys finish up!" he shouts through the house. "We'll be in the shower!" I'm deposited in the cubicle, fully dressed as the warm water clears my eyesight, and Lucas crowds me against the tile. "Fuck, I can't wait until tomorrow night." He's beaming, and I run through my schedule. Surely fajita Friday isn't a big enough deal to be on the Thorn's radar. Then it dawns on me.

"The sports rally?" I raise a brow.

"Yeah, that too. But tomorrow night, we're publicly announcing you as our new Pet." Lucas cups my cheek just as my jaw drops. I forget how to breathe. Tomorrow? So soon? Sensing my hesitation, Lucas works his hands down the t-shirt sticking to my skin. He plays with the hem whilst I try to plead with my wide eyes.

"Can't things just stay as they are?" Things are good. Better than good, they're perfect. I don't understand why we have to mess it all up.

"Sophia," Lucas breathes my name. It's as foreign to me as the serious expression he gives. "You're turning my world upside down and driving me stir crazy. I'm ready to scream it from the rooftops, to let the world know who you belong to." I sigh against his chest. This is their world. The limelight, the tabloids, the publicity. I just hope I'll be able to keep up once all of the other girls are cursing me behind my back. Peering around, I notice the brass shower head has been pushed high up to accommodate someone taller than Lucas' height, the glass doors still open by a slither at his back.

"Is this...Kyan's room?" I tilt my head at the large, over the counter mirror. Lucas grins, his gaze feral as his shoulders draw up into a shrug.

"He has the biggest shower." Lucas raises his arm slightly, and I take my cue to duck. I need some air, some space to settle my thundering heart. His strong arms wrap around my waist, and he proceeds to strip me out of the clothes with finesse. The sopping wet t-shirt and sweatpants hit the floor, quickly followed by his apron and boxers. There's no denying him, and if this is one of the last times we're together secretively, I'm going to damn well enjoy it.

I arch my back from the cool tiles, my nipples taut. My lips are parted, waiting for a kiss that doesn't come. Instead, Lucas purposely brushes his solid cock against my lower stomach and reaches past me. His hand on my hip turns me slowly. I press my hands on the tile and jut my ass out.

"Fuck, you're so eager," Lucas whispers into my ear, his hot breath tingling down my spine. He brushes the water-soaked hair from my face and starts lathering shampoo through my hair. I open my mouth on a gasp to tell him I need a special type of shampoo to keep the blue coloring in my hair, but then I saw the bottle. It's mine. I bite down on my lip, my heart pounding in anticipation.

Instead of going where I thought, Lucas takes his time, massaging my scalp and I'm lost to another type of pleasure. I close my eyes, losing myself to the soothing rhythm of his hands moving in sync with the water cascading down my body. Sighs are drawn from my mouth, his fingers working some kind of magic as they apply just enough pressure to make my limbs weak. He uses this momentum, pushing me down onto my knees. Angled away from the spray, Lucas watches me eye up his shaft, which stands proud in front of my face.

Suddenly, the door swings open, and Ezra steps in sporting an uncaring grin. "Room for one more?" he asks, already pulling off his shorts and tossing them aside. He grips my chin, drawing my attention to his thick cock instead.

"I wasn't interrupting anything, was I?" Ezra teases, stepping under the stream of warm water. Droplets pound from his back while I sit in his shadow, peering up with large eyes.

"Yup," Lucas sighs. He unhooks the shower head, bringing it close to wash the shampoo from my hair. I shiver, despite the heat, looking between the pair to see who will beat this battle of wills. Then I remember I don't have to wait. I'm not a simple submissive.

Gripping both of their shafts, matching hisses are drawn from above. Lucas falters on washing my hair, awkwardly fumbling to put the shower head back in place as I drag my tongue over his tip. I match the movement with Ezra, curling my tongue at the end. He grins and pulls me closer. Like for like, I lick one while smoothly stroking my hand along the other. Movement catches the corner of my eye.

"Oh, don't let me stop you," Kyan watches on from across the room. Having abandoned his apron and mixing bowl, he's sitting on the counter. His knuckles are white from where he grips the edge, his face as strained as the dick in his boxers. I swallow thickly. *Three at once. Piercings.*

Ezra takes full advantage of my distraction to tug my jaw open and thrust himself inside. I moan around him, sending vibrations up his length as he runs his fingers through my wet hair. His touch is like praise, urging me to open up and take him deeper. Lucas grows impatient, gripping my neck and pulling me off his brother with a pop. Then it's his turn.

Warmth seeps into my side as Kyan slides across the wet floor. The water has turned tepid, but none of us care. I'm not giving the reprieve by Ezra or Lucas to look his way, but the cotton of his boxers brushes against my thigh. My spine relaxes. He's still wearing his boxers. Of all the guys, Kyan is the one I'm most worried about unleashing himself on me.

Fingers stroke my arms, my shoulders, and round to my breasts. Kyan kneads and teases, placing kisses everywhere his fingers have been. His touch has a fire lighting within, and I take the newfound lust out on Ezra's cock. Sucking him hard, he groans and leans his head back against the tile. When I do the same to Lucas, Kyan's fingers find my clit.

We're a mess of moans and passion. Kyan rubs me in small circles as his other hand eases in from the back. Skating over my ass, I clench. He chuckles, sliding two fingers into me with ease. His mouth is on my jaw now, kissing and sucking. Similar welts have been left across my neck. There won't be any hiding the bruises; I'm marked for all to see.

As Kyan's fingers impale me harder and those rubbing my clit become more insistent, I focus using my mouth on Ezra. He's the closest, his groans growing louder, his hand tearing the hair at my scalp. He holds me still, thrusting into my open mouth until I gag. Tears spring to my eyes as I peer into his icy gaze.

"Cry for me, beautiful. Cry while my cock explodes in that pretty little mouth." Tears slip from my eyes, which seems to be his undoing. Thumping into the back of my throat, I'm merely an instrument for him to use. Absentmindedly, I've been gripping Lucas firmly and pumping him with the same vigor as Ezra's thrusts. He pulls out of me, his hand on my jaw forcing my mouth to stay open.

"Tongue out," Lucas grits through his teeth. I obey just as they both come for me, exploding across my face. I continue to drive their orgasms forward, my hands moving in complete unison on both of their shafts. Their groans are music to my ears, but Kyan isn't satisfied until mine are just as loud. Adding a third finger inside of me, his arm wounds my waist to save me from falling over. He pushes his digits in, twists and repeats, faster and faster until I'm also screaming, clamping down on his hand. He's pressed against my back, mimicking my strained inhales as if they were his own.

"I think I'm going to keep you." He says it so softly, I'm not sure he even knows it was out loud. All three of us come down while Kyan's cock pulses at my back. The water of the shower is on my face once more, hands working together to clean me off their mess. My hair will need washing again, and Lucas is already reaching for the shampoo.

"Somehow, I don't quite think this picnic is going to happen." I sag against Kyan's body. He's taut, strained with need but makes no move to proposition me further.

"Oh, it's happening," Lucas chuckles, wiping my cheeks clean. "I just forgot to mention you're the main dish."

***

We ate the Eton Mess bites in bed that evening, and they were glorious.

## Chapter 21

Clinking our glasses together, Letty and I down pomegranate mojitos before she finishes painting my face. Standing behind, Jess continues to braid my hair, giving me the full Waversea cheerleader look. Her vanity mirror has been turned away to not spoil the surprise. Giggling and music swirl around the pale pink and cream decor, several girls dancing while they change. There are easily twelve of Letty's friends in her sorority bedroom, making the huge suite seem small.

"All done," Letty smiles at her handiwork. Her strawberry blonde hair is pulled tight into two chunky braids, a yellow crop top, and a black mini skirt exposing her athletic body. Planting my backpack in my lap, she nudges her head as if to say 'scram,' so she can start painting her next victim.

I slink away, seeking out the bathroom for a moment of peace. My cheeks hurt from smiling, my social meter already ticking past 'filled'. Closing the door, I rest against it and sigh.

"*So, are you going to wear it?*" Jazzie's voice rings in my head before I open my eyes. She's sprawled in the bathtub, her biker boots crossed at the ankles. Casually looking at the backpack clutched in my hands, she blows a bubble of gum. I know what she's referring to.

Dropping the bag on the counter, I pick out the red ribbon box. No one was home when I retreated back to Thorn Manor after class, but this box was waiting for me on my bed.

'*Last minute practice before the game. See you there, and wear this. L. x*'

I peer inside for the second time. The lingerie is exquisite, unlike anything I've ever seen before. Split into three pieces, the bra, corseted middle, and panties are crafted from black lace in a flower design. The shoulder straps and back of the thong are fine threads of diamonds, matching those which crisscross over the stomach.

"*Well?*" Jazzie prompts. I roll my eyes.

"Of course I'm going to wear it." I swallow hard. Stripping, I pull on the underwear, cinching my waist as tight as I am able in the corset. The lace kisses my skin, rubbing in all the right places to tantalize me all evening. Thicker rose motifs cover somewhat of my modesty, at the apex of my thighs and over my nipples.

Braving a look in the mirror, my cheeks flush. I look completely different, starting with the absence of my glasses. Letty insisted on contacts to save ruining her face paint–twin lines of swirling dots around my eyes in the team's colors. My hair has been braided on either side of my head, the top gelled up into a mohawk which floats down my back. My fingers toy with the edge of the lace against my stomach, hardly recognizing my own body.

"You nearly ready, Sophia?" Letty bangs and asks through the door, causing me to jolt.

"Yes, just coming!" I shout back, quickly grabbing the rest of my clothes from my bag. Tugging on skinny jeans, I then shrug on a yellow blouse which struggles to close around my now-pronounced cleavage. I slowly button the front, watching my secret lingerie become concealed. I take a moment to tug the cuffs down at my wrists, making sure my scar is tucked away from public view. The brothers are the only ones who have seen it, and I'm still not comfortable with that. Then I stuff my feet into my white Converse. Alongside the gift box, a pair of black heels had been provided, and I decided to leave them behind. No, thank you blisters on my first game night. The music cuts out as I open the door and blend into the exiting crowd, following their parade of laughter all the way to the sports arena.

Posters line the sidewalk, cheering emanating from ahead. I force myself to follow, despite all instincts screaming to run away. If the crowds weren't enough to make me feel claustrophobic, the thought of this 'public claiming' has my gut tightening in knots. Is it going to be as medieval as it sounds? Perhaps it was foolish of me to avoid asking, because now the unknown is threatening to suffocate me from inside.

The path curves around the back of the building, avoiding the open field I was running through two weeks ago. So much has changed in such a short space of time. I'm either a horny fool or a gullible idiot. Striding towards the rear parking lot, an entrance appears beyond parked coaches. Both have Radley spray painted across the sides.

The sound of drums pounds through my being as I step over the threshold, my lungs seizing at the sheer amount of people present. The bleachers are packed, the crowd split into yellow and red. Homemade banners are thrust into the air, a mixture of booing and cheering making my head spin. In the center of the court, a referee and an umpire appear with microphones, their voices booming through speakers.

"Ladies and gentlemen!" the first shouts. Letty grabs my hand, tugging me towards the stairs. "Welcome to the most anticipated Sports Rally so far this year! Prepare yourselves to witness an exciting clash between these two talented teams. It's sure to be a thrilling game filled with passion, skill, and determination." Another round of cheers is punctuated by drummers parading around the edge of the court. "Put your hands together to welcome our competitors, Rrrradleyyyy!"

Cheerleaders accompany the players leaking from the far side of the court, their jerseys black and red. Many have red stripes through their hair, and all have fists pumping in the sky as they break apart to goad the crowd. Being tugged towards a seat at the end of a row, I don't know where to look. Color and noise assault me so that none of the voices in my head can bleed through. It's only when the umpire speaks again and the crowd lessens their roars, do I hear the Cheshire cat laughing.

Large eyes and a stripy tail appear before me, spinning and twirling towards the court. Diverting to a corner I hadn't previously seen, he lays upon a gold and red throne as the Warriors are announced. And there they are, in all their glory. As if they command the light, Kyan, Lucas, and Ezra shine brighter than any of the other players as they run out onto the court to a deafening cheer. And rightly so, because they're freaking gorgeous. A perfect mix of blonde, black, and auburn hair, the definition of tanned muscle and chiseled jaws. Letty once described them as gods, and I can see why.

"Fuck, they are so hot," Jess looks over to fan herself. From beside me, Letty sighs.

"I'd give my left tit to be their pet. I wonder who the lucky bitch is." Keeping my gaze forward, I slink into the seat, hoping the brothers won't be able to pick me out. This was a terrible idea. What the hell was I thinking?! All I wanted was a quiet life in a new school, to leave my past and my delusions behind. Making friends would have been an added bonus, and I'm about to blow that too.

"You know what," I mutter to Letty, "I actually feel kinda sick. Might be the mojito disagreeing with me. I'm going to grab some fresh air." Letty's eyes fill with concern but she nods, letting me slink down the steps towards the exit. Using the distraction of those hollering and swaying banners around, I make it all the way to the bottom step and round the banister. Then I feel it. The hairs rise on the back of my neck, the weight of attention searing the back of my head.

Frozen to the spot, all I manage is to look over my shoulder and see those three pairs of haunted eyes on me. Only Lucas smiles, his sneakers eating up the space between us. With his attention, comes that of the entire audience and the umpire.

"Hold up, folks, we have one more announcement which needs to be made!" *No, no, no, no, god fuck no.* I make a run for it, but Lucas is too fast. He's always too fast. His hand grabs my arm, whirling me against his chest as the other two appear to block me in.

"Where are you going, Sophia?" Kyan asks at the same time Lucas speaks.

"Where's the outfit I gave you?" Shuddering, goosebumps line my skin as his green gaze tracks my cleavage. "Oh, Feisty One, the time for hiding is over." Hands seize me, tearing at my clothes until I'm left standing in the diamond-embedded lingerie.

"Please, no, not my blouse," I squirm, knowing it's useless. The hideous scar on my arm is laid bare for all to see. My words are lost to the cheers. No one can hear me over the wolf whistles, and even if they could, no one would help. This is a game to them all. A cheerleader steps forward with a pair of black Jimmy Choos in her hands.

"Told you she wouldn't wear the heels," Ezra growls, accepting them and kneeling. Numbly, I allow him to remove my sneakers and guide my feet into the shoes, putting me six inches closer to Lucas' gaze. A strip of leather is threaded around my neck, tightened as the collar seals my fate, and I merely stand there.

"Why are you doing this to me?" I ask quietly, tears filling my vision. He reads my lips and frowns. Genuine hurt passes his features as the umpire announces me for the entire school to see.

"The newest, and last there will ever be, welcome the Thorn Brother's Pet!" The crowd goes crazy with a mix of cheers, boos and then, there's Letty and her girls. Braving a look in their direction, they're stunned, gaping. I shy away, letting Kyan slip his arm into mine as Lucas takes the other side, Ezra up front holding the leash high for all to see. I'm led over to the throne. The courtside seat where I am to remain on display in my lingerie for everyone to see. Clearly, the feminist movement didn't reach this corner of the state.

My ass grazes the velvet purple cushioning, my knee crossing over the other and my back rigidly straight. There are two lessons I took from my time at juvie. First, show no fear. Even when you're dying inside from self-hatred or humiliation, you can't let anyone know. The second is in the act of zoning out. Multiple characters instantly appear at my distress, barricading the court from sight. Even as the umpire reels off rules and a booming klaxon sounds for the game to begin, Jazzie is laying her head on my lap.

*Could have been worse*, she tries to reason.

*Dude*, another figure scowls, planting a hand on my knee. She's new and looks intriguingly like Letty. "*They stripped her and left her here to be gawked at. I wouldn't be surprised if people started throwing tomatoes.*"

*These aren't their rules, remember. The previous Pets orchestrated all of this,* Jazzie stands, blocking the view of the hoop, which was scored in the first two minutes. *All they want is to share a lover and not be ridiculed for it.*

I don't look away from her. The alternative is to let my gaze drift towards the stands. No doubt, Letty is feeling beyond betrayed. There goes my newfound friends and seat at the canteen table. I'll have to bring my claws for English Lit on Monday morning. I don't do well being backed into a corner, and a violent lashing out is on the horizon.

*Save it for those it should be directed at, honey,* the new girl leans on Jazzie. I don't know her name yet, but I have respect for the 'Kill the Cunts' banner she's holding. My nostrils flare. She's right. I'll save my anger for the Thorn Brothers, let it fester until the right moment. No matter who decided this throne stunt was a good idea, they know me. They knew I'd hate it, that it would have a damaging effect on my self-esteem, and they did it anyway. Drumming my fingernails on the throne arm, I sit back, becoming enveloped in my fantasies.

Outside of my protective bubble, chaos reigns. My head thrums with sound, a rogue commentator nearby relaying back the game I refuse to watch. The Waversea Warriors aren't working together as well as usual, and maybe it has something to do with their key players being distracted.

Radley, however, are on full form thanks to a new captain. I hear this all, yet I couldn't care less.

Instead, I drown out everyone. Those in reality, those in my mind. Before my eyes, I will the room to transform. Vines coil around the basket poles, thick with thorns and pulsing with purple roses. Bark, akin to the muesli the brothers eat every morning, ripples across the court's flooring, softening the sound of sneakers hitting the wood. From the bleachers, a canopy of trees lurches forward, distancing me from the arena but also filling it with shadows. Pockets of darkness which I use to tuck away all those in my eyeline. This is where my talent flares. Where I can wrap myself in a safety blanket and leave my troubles far behind.

Time drifts by, the numbness in my limbs barely resonating. I'm too preoccupied watching a butterfly flutter past, dancing with a squirrel hanging on a low-baring branch. The next klaxon, which echoes around the arena, doesn't even make me flinch, my senses dulled to my true surroundings.

"Half time," Ezra smacks my thigh and grabs the leash. "Get your ass back here."

## Chapter 22

Tugging me along by the leash, my eyes are hazy, unable to catch up. I've slipped too far, false imagery lingering on the edge of my vision as I look around. Lucas and Kyan are right behind. Stumbling into the locker room, the door is slammed closed with the rest of the team outside. The quietness inside somehow hurts my ears even more than the arena, like a ringing I can't stifle. Then I remember where I am. Who I'm with. At the first opportunity, I rip the leash from Ezra's hand and tear the collar off.

"Did you all enjoy that?" I shove at his chest, kicking off my shoes. "Objectifying me?!" Another shove has his back hitting the lockers. "Am I just some joke to you?!" Arms grab me from behind, but I keep my glare on Ezra. He's so much easier to be angry at because I know Lucas hasn't just upset me. He's hurt me. As if I didn't mean anything to him at all.

"Calm down," Kyan grunts, pinning my arms back. Red coats my vision like a raging bull is released within. Doubling my efforts, I kick Ezra in the skin, wishing I'd left my heels on.

"Why would you choose me for this bullshit? Pick any other whore with no self-respect. I never wanted this. Now the entire school has seen me in my underwear, sitting on the sidelines like a court jester." My nostrils flare as I'm dragged backward and forced to sit in Kyan's lap on the bench.

"That's not...," Lucas appears, running a hand through his auburn hair. "It wasn't like that."

"Oh really? Please enlighten me—what was it like?" There it is again, in his green eyes. That same flash of hurt from earlier. I hate it when he doesn't smile, but it's not my job to placate him.

"The throne is in our direct eye line. We wanted to show you off," Lucas mumbles, his hands raised in defeat. I'm not buying it.

"As your slutty pet," I scowl. Ezra darts forward, gripping my chin and twisting my face upwards.

"As our Queen, you idiot. Having you there bolsters us, makes us feel special to have the most exquisite woman in the room as close to the court as possible, and her attention is *supposed* to be on us." I stop struggling, the air knocked from my lungs. In my peripheral vision, all of the female characters who plague me are shaking their heads, and had those words come from the others, I may have been able to convince myself they were lying. But Ezra? Ezra hasn't doesn't tell me what I want to hear. He doesn't do *sweet*, and I doubt he'd start now if it weren't true.

"We didn't mean to ridicule you," Kyan adds softly beside my ear. "We only want to..."

"To?" I push when no one continues.

"Worship you," Lucas answers, kneeling before me. "The second we graduate, I'm being shipped off to be married. I don't get to date, to feel butterflies, to enjoy the cat-and-mouse flirtation game. This is the extent of my relationships."

He toys with the diamond straps at my shoulders as Kyan's hold on my arms loosens. Ezra's blue eyes soften for the first time, his hand resting on Lucas' shoulder. This is what they live for. The three of them, brothers of pure survival who will do whatever it takes to remain bonded. Including dating together, and screwing together.

"That's what this has all been about," I breathe as understanding dawns. Lucas nods, and even Ezra joins him on the floor.

"I wanted to feel as connected to my brothers as possible until I leave and to have fun. The pet thing was a simple solution. Girls usually jump at the chance, and...I'll admit, it got kinda out of hand. No one has ever fought against us before. No one has been like you," he brushes a hand over my cheek. "You're unique, special. You make us work harder, and the reward is so much sweeter. I'm so glad you're the one we get to have this last experience with."

I have no fight left. He should have told me, but again–would I have believed him? That the rich kid who could have anything, anyone in the world, wanted me? Leaning forward, my forehead connects with Lucas', a sigh filling my chest.

"Alright," I whisper, my usual lack of trust seeping away. It holds no ground against Lucas' sincerity. He's so open, bared to me. "I surrender. I'm all yours. All of yours." His green eyes flicker with relief, and a smile graces his lips. Not the smug one he reserves for humiliation, but a genuine smile that melts my core. Ezra and Kyan echo the sentiment, their bodies relaxing. The tension in the air dissipates. I understand fully now what this is all about. How it helps to bond them to each other, but also to me. We're one now, and I belong with them.

Before I can think any further, Lucas reaches out, a gentle hand cradling my face as he draws me closer. His breath is warm against my skin, his eyes holding an intensity which causes my heart to stutter in my chest. The moment stretches between us until his lips finally find mine. I moan, the height of hesitation and desire crashing down on me. All that's left is the softness of Lucas' lips, which feels like a plea and promise all rolled into one, entering us into new territory. I'm becoming their equal.

Ezra strokes my legs, never going above the knee. Beneath me, Kyan's hips roll, his hands exploring my body. Starting at my shoulders, his palms carve a path south, over my biceps and to the crook of my elbows. My mouth stops moving against Lucas', my world coming to a sudden halt.

"Trust me," Kyan mutters into my ear. I don't relax, but I don't stop him either. His hands raise to hover just above my skin as they descend over my forearms. Lucas cups my cheek, drawing my tongue out of my mouth with a flick of his. I try to indulge him, but I'm distracted by Kyan's hand stalling directly over my scar, steadily pressing down. Another hand joins his, and then the third. I don't know why I expected it to happen any other way.

"You're so beautiful, Sophia," Kyan tells me. "Every part of you." I twist my mouth away from Lucas, peering down at the hands rounding my arm. They aren't squeezing, but there's enough pressure there to make my lip wobble.

"I hate that scar. I hate what it reminds me of." A lump forms in my throat. Ezra kneels up higher, his jaw brushing mine the way a lion would greet his lioness.

"Not all wounds leave scars and the ones that do mean we've been forged into something better. Stronger." Leaning back an inch, Ezra's blue eyes bore into mine with more vulnerability than I've ever seen. "You're so strong, Sophia."

When they shift their hands, I don't even gasp. My eyes are captivated by Ezra's as Kyan plays with my blue hair. Strong isn't a word I associate with myself, especially since I've met the Thorns. All I've shown is weakness. Desperation for my meds, relying on them to keep me calm. But no more. I want to be the version of myself these boy believe me to be. When they brush their fingers over my scar this time, I don't shy away. Each motion is full of reverence; slow, meaningful strokes that speak louder than any words could.

"Time's up!" A banging sounds on the door. Fuck, the game. The crowds. No one inside the locker room moves. There's a silent exchange between us four, an exchange of acceptance and trust. I shudder beneath the weight of their palms, knowing I needed this to move forward. The Thorn Brothers aren't just a distraction for the time being. They're setting me up with the tools to tackle life after we've all moved on to new ventures.

"I'm truly sorry about the throne," Lucas breathes.

"You don't have to go back out there," Ezra adds.

"We can get you an escort home. Keep our relationship a secret, the way you prefer?" Kyan leans his head against mine. At the back of the room, Jazzie appears against the lockers, smirking.

*They chose you to be their last because there's no replacing you.* I smile in her direction, pushing up to my feet. Retrieving the collar and heels, I re-dress myself how they wanted me.

"Are you guys kidding me? This Queen has an appearance to make, and her boyfriends have a game to win." I offer the leash to Ezra. Slowly standing, the three of them develop matching smiles of pride.

"We've never been called boyfriends before," Kyan chuckles.

"I like it," Lucas winds his arm around my waist. I giggle, deciding I like it too. It's a narrative I can get behind; no contracts or rules necessary. Ezra tugs the leash lightly, starting our walk towards the door.

The three of them are banded around me when we stride back onto the court. This time, no boos greet us. Not that I hear, anyway. I tune out everything except for the gentle strokes against my arms and thighs. Let people stare, let them be disgusted. As degrading as this seems, as twisted and fucked up, I can do this for the Thorns. For Lucas. For the sacrifice he's making, being betrothed upon graduation, I can give him this. Hell, for the next several weeks, I'll be the Pet they didn't realize they've been missing this entire time. I am their Queen, after all.

## Chapter 23

"Allow me," Kyan offers his hand. I smile, stepping down from the throne, which has been mounted in the back of a pick-up truck. After the Waversea Warriors took the win, I was paraded back to Thorn Manor with my champions around my feet. Even I have to admit, it was exhilarating waving to the cheering crowds who followed, whilst multiple hands stroked my calves. Amongst all of these people, I'm still their focus.

Attempting to hop down from the truck, Ezra swoops in to toss me over his shoulder, ass in the air. The cheers grow louder, accompanying us all the way to the front door until they're shut out. Planting me down on the heels, Ezra crowds me against the nearest wall, his body radiating heat through the dark. He prefers it this way, I decide. Concealed within shadows, anonymous outlines that rely on touch and base instinct. I feel his breath on my neck as he leans down, his lips dangerously close to mine. The cheers of the crowd have faded away, and all I can hear is my own ragged breath and the beat of my heart.

Reaching up to my face, his fingers trail my jawline, stopping at my chin. I'm trapped, caught in his all-consuming presence, unable to break away. Ezra, the man I've yet to truly connect with. The one I offered myself in the library to and got rejected. There's no denying the electricity between us now, the tension building until it's almost unbearable.

"Just fucking kiss her already, or I will," Lucas comments from somewhere within the adjoining room. On a muffled groan, Ezra's lips crash down on mine, and I'm lost. Lost to the feeling of his mouth, lost in the sensation from the rough claim of his tongue. I wrap my arms around his neck, pulling him closer, inviting him in deeper. Ezra's hands roam down my body, pulling my hips into his. I gasp as he grinds his solid length against me, those silk sports shorts doing nothing to conceal his arousal. It works to stir my own higher, and suddenly—I want him.

I want Ezra to take me right here, rewrite everything I thought I knew about myself, and piece me back together. My fingers tangle in his blond hair, pulling him into me encouragingly. His heart pounds against my own, his hands sliding up my stomach to my breasts. I arch into his touch, my body begging for more.

"Warm her up for us, Ez," Kyan slaps him hard on the back, breaking our trance. "We need to shower."

"What he means is," I turn Ezra's face back to me, refusing to let our moment be ruined. Not when we've waited this long for it. "Make me come at least twice before they get back."

*That's my girl*, Jazzie mutters in the background. I feel her drifting away from me, withdrawing into a tiny box in my brain where she and the others belong.

I'm quickly distracted from that thought, as Ezra picks me up and walks me through the house. Between strides, his lips seek out mine over and over. Unable to resist the insatiable taste of danger. Each touch tells me he wants everything I've got to give and more. No words are said. None are needed. We're both one with the moment, our bodies begging for more.

My back is lowered onto a mattress. As he continues his exploration of my lingerie, I release a quiet moan, the sound swallowed by his mouth. Coming to rest his warm palms on my hips, he lowers himself over me, the hard line of his erection against my stomach.

Pushing the shorts past his erection, I grab his length and stroke him in my palm. Ezra lets out a muffled sound, his tongue flicking against my neck. Coiling his fingers against the thin lace between my thighs, he tugs it aside to find me soaking from anticipation. The pad of his thumb is instantly in place, barely moving as he circles my clit. I shudder beneath his touch, reeling for more. He stops, a rare smile gracing his face as he denies me.

"Please, Ezra," I whimper, wanting to feel him in other places. I squirm in the hopes for added friction. "Give me more."

"Not a chance," he slowly shakes his head. "You're so fucking hot like this." Eyes hooded, chest panting, I shake my head.

"Fine, have it your way." Rolling out from under him, Ezra doesn't try to stop me. I stand and walk over to the chair, similar to the one I have in the corner of my room, preparing to give Ezra a strip show, starting with my corset. His arms move to settle beneath his head as my fingers delicately pop the clasps at the back. One by one, until the threaded diamonds are dismantled, and the middle scrap of lace falls away. I hook my fingers into the sides of my thong, rolling my hips in time with the music in my head. Slowly pushing them down my thighs, I can't help but stare at the man reclined on the bed.

He's a mixture of the asshole I thought I knew and the Dom I've come to understand–someone who can control my body with a flick of his wrist, a lick of his tongue. His icy blue eyes are hungry, his teeth sinking into his bottom lip.

The door handle turns, becoming stuck and a round of banging pounds on the other side of the wood.

"The fuck, Ez? Open up!" Lucas shouts, and my mouth drops open. He's locked us inside.

"Please, continue," Ezra tilts his head. His begging sounds so similar to my own just a moment ago, and it's my turn to smirk.

"Not a chance," I echo back. "You look so fucking hot like this–with blue balls, I mean." Striding for the door, I pop the lock before Ezra manages to catch me, his arms banding around my middle. Lucas bursts inside, Kyan right behind with towels bunched at their waists. A fight takes place, my feet swept from the floor as Ezra jumps up on the bed and uses me as a barricade. The others join a second later, their towels forgotten and cocks half-mast. A glint of silver catches my eye from Kyan's particular region.

"She's mine!" Ezra shouts, taking me by surprise. Lucas lunges first, trying to pry me free, while Kyan attacks Ezra from behind. Biceps bunch around my head until suddenly, we're freefalling onto the mattress. Laughter spills, limbs tangle. Amongst the damp skin and wandering hands, a mouth finds mine. The atmosphere turns heated in an instant, no more stalling as my breasts are pried free from the bra and my thighs are widened.

Clouding my vision, Lucas' green eyes remain on mine, his tongue swirling around my mouth. In the background, I vaguely hear the vibrations before my clit is blessed with the pulsing rhythm of a wand. I arch and groan, Lucas not giving me a moment's reprieve. This is how they like me, lost to the passion and unaware of what they're planning on doing next. Delving into the kiss, the heated chase of tongues, nibbling teeth, and bruising lips, Ezra makes a strangled sound from between my legs.

"Focus on me, baby. I was instructed to give at least two orgasms before the real fun begins." He doesn't play around either, ramping up the vibrations and lazily pushing his fingers inside of me, twisting and tugging down. He doesn't have to wait for my first one, the anticipation is too much to bear. For the second, Ezra replaces the wand with his tongue, and his fingers trail further back. Toying with my ass, I tense, suddenly remembering this is it. The night I take all three, and I'm not sure I'm ready.

"Relax," Kyan murmurs beside my ear. It's him teasing my nipples, pinching to the point of pain, and then rubbing the aching pebbles across his palm. Lucas senses the change in my body, releasing me from our kiss to prop himself beside me.

"You're ready," Lucas reassures, stroking along my jawline to the base of my throat.

"And if you're not, we'll stop," Kyan adds. Ezra, his face buried in my pussy, mutters something incoherent, which I can only imagine is a–'no, we fucking won't.' I should be assured, but my thighs tighten, risking cutting off Ezra's air supply. All three of them, at once, inside of me. Chewing on my bottom lip, Kyan pries it free.

"What are you scared of, baby?"

"Your...um, your piercing," I whisper, flames heating my cheeks. If Ezra wasn't pinning me down, I'd probably run away and lock myself in a closet somewhere. Kyan chuckles, shifting to kneel beside me. And there it is, or rather–they are. On the underside of his shaft, a solid metal bar through the gland beneath his plump purple head has two small balls on either side.

"This is the frenum," he shows me, nudging the bar with his thumb. This cock is a thing of beauty, silky smooth and free of any foreskin. His hand travels south. "And this is the lorum," Kyan strokes the horizontal bar at the base of his shaft and the top of his balls. "Nothing to be scared of. Here, let me show you."

Reaching for my head, Lucas lifts my upper back and nudges himself underneath, propping me up as Kyan guides his dick into my mouth. The cold metal of his piercing touches my tongue, aided by the salty musk of arousal radiating from his shaft. We've only just begun, yet he's ready to have me, to take me in any capacity I'm prepared to give. His length is hard against my lips, yet he moves slowly and carefully, allowing me time to adjust. As I take him further in, I feel the metal bar hit the back of my throat as the second one slides across my tongue. Not painful or as intrusive as I imagined. A gentle stroke, an added sensation I can only imagine will drive me crazy inside my pussy. I groan, his cock vibrating within my throat.

"Not so bad, right?" Kyan asks. I don't answer, Ezra commanding my attention once more. Sucking my clit hard, a finger sinks into my ass. A moment of pain and blind panic are quickly chased away by the pleasure he brings. Instead of retracting, Ezra's finger spins, rotates, teases. I tremble, my body no longer my own.

With Lucas's focus on removing my bra and toying with my nipples, the sensation of having three men pleasing me at the same time is overwhelming. Kyan's piercing rubs against my tongue as I move my head up and down, growing bolder, exploring the different textures and sensations that can be created from his body. Ezra's experienced fingers work their magic between my legs with a combination of expert teasing and gentle caresses, making me moan uncontrollably in pleasure. Every inch of Kyan fills my mouth as he begins thrusting deeper and deeper, enticed by the humming. I am so lost in the moment that nothing else matters but pleasure. Mine, theirs, ours. My commitment to being their pet drives me even wilder.

My orgasm rips through me so intensely, my scream is stifled by dick. Kyan's breathing becomes more labored as I suck hard, riding through the intensity as if my life depends on it. Waves of coursing pleasure take over my body, causing me to jerk and flinch uncontrollably. Lucas holds me in place, Ezra not relenting until I go slack. Then I fall back on Lucas, the remaining trembles leaving a blissful tingle through my entire body.

"That makes two," Ezra kneels upright. If I thought they'd give me a moment to catch my breath, I couldn't have been more wrong. I'm flipped, dragged, and repositioned over Lucas' cock. I know the drill by now, I am to suck the monstrosity before me until I can't breathe whilst trying to contain myself from giving in to these boys too easily. These men are skilled in sexual torture and advocates of my darkest fantasies. Making himself comfortable against the headboard, Lucas shifts his legs horizontally, giving Kyan room to slide beneath me. Ezra is at the rear, standing at the foot of the bed and stroking my ass.

"Do you still hate us, Sophia?" Kyan asks, toying with my nipples. I groan.

"So, so much," I lie, still too conscious of appearing weak. Too aware I'm one in a long list of Pets. I want to be different. I want to make *them* work for it, force them to remember me.

"Good." Ezra spanks me so harshly, I cry out and ruin my unaffected facade. "Hate-fucks are so much better." I hear the bottle of lube being opened, but it's Kyan who has my attention.

Gently holding my hips, he lifts and lowers me over his jutting cock. His touch is electric, sending shivers down my spine as I surrender to his offered embrace. Arms band around my back, his muscles creating a cage of comfort while his dick slides into me. I'm wet enough, even without Ezra's lubed fingers circling and sliding into my ass. Those piercings add a heady sensation, my cunt so completely filled, I'm sure there's no room for Ezra as he lines up with my ass. Again, so, so wrong.

Ezra makes room, driving me further into Kyan's hold. I bite down on his collar bone, withholding a scream. It's too much, too intense. Pain twinges with a burning that makes my eyes water, but once fully seethed, Ezra stills. It's up to Kyan to roll his hips, sending all three of us into a frenzy. Strained groans fill the room, the most incredible feeling uniting and twisting through the three of us. We're caught in the euphoria of the moment, lost in each other's passion, but there's someone missing.

Kyan reads my mind, gripping my ribs to stretch me further up the bed. My nipple slips into his mouth with ease, and Lucas watches the scene like his favorite porno. Stroking his cock, his green eyes consume me. Licking my lips, with two cocks filling me, I eagerly take Lucas into my mouth. All three at once. Jazzie would be so proud. There's no time for delusions now, my mind too distracted by the silky shaft easing into the back of my throat as if it was molded to fit.

"Tell us how it feels to be ours," Lucas demands, driving into my mouth harder. His words take me as much by surprise as the intrusion. I clench my teeth together, stilling his thrusts whilst refusing myself from falling any harder. They can have my body, make me more vulnerable than any other, but my mind is my own. Realizing I wouldn't answer, even if he did withdraw his cock and allow me to do so, Lucas smirks.

"Fair enough, I'll go first. You're insatiable. The perfect fit, the perfect choice. No one has suited us all this well before. Right, Ez?"

"Damn fucking right," Ezra says with a pained grunt. Not physically pained, but the type of blissful torture one feels when teetering on the edge. I know because I'm right there with him.

"So fucking perfect," Kyan agrees. Moving on to my other nipple, his expert hands massage my breasts and slip down towards my clit. I quickly slap him away. I can't handle any more, not when his steady pace is hurtling me towards a climax which will shatter us all.

My heart picks up a beat. Kyan's hot breath fans my neck. With every kiss he places against my collarbone, I float higher. Drift further from my body when I'm no longer overwhelmed by the fullness but at one with it. With them. Kyan's hips roll in a perfect rhythm to the bobbing of my head. Lucas moans softly. Ezra holds firm, his cock a dull weight pushing against all the right places. All moving together in perfect harmony.

The stirrings of my orgasm intensify. Expert fingers explore every inch of my body, cupping my breasts before moving downwards to stroke my clit in tantalizing circles. I slip into a state of pure ecstasy, lost to the energy building around us. Every muscle in my body is ready to explode, my back arching as the pleasure becomes too much to contain. This is what we needed. A moment to solidify this connection. My skin pricks with electricity as hard bodies press against mine. With a final sharp thrust from Kyan, I suck Lucas hard. So hard, my cheeks hollow out as stars flare behind my eyes.

I'm hit with an orgasm that knocks the air from my lungs with its force. Ezra growls, cumming inside of my ass. The pulsing of his cock spurs on my own screams. Still pumping warm cum, he slowly withdraws, the release as pleasurable as the entry. I tilt my hips back, calling a mixture of their names when I'm flipped on my back.

Kyan's weight presses down onto my chest, my legs held wide at the ankles by Lucas and Ezra. Increasing his pace, Kyan fucks me. So hard, so deep, I'm certain he's pounding directly into my soul. My orgasm triples, drawn out with the ferocious slamming of his cock. I'm soaking, screaming, and spent by the time Kyan whips out, coming into a discarded towel.

Just as I moan, fighting to catch my breath, a warm tongue licks my pussy. Strokes my clit. Looking down, I find both Lucas and Ezra cleaning me of my own cum, multiple hands pinning down my thighs. I buck regardless, rasping for words. When they fail, I reach out and run my fingers through their hair.

"You taste so good, Feisty." Lucas smirks at me, green eyes twinkling. "Do you like having two men lick your pussy?"

"Yes." I bite my lip as my cheeks flame red.

"Good girl." Ezra grins. Sighing and content, I rest back, savoring the hot strokes they provide. A soft caress. A loving brush. Conformation they care for me. I've been waiting for this.

We remain there for what feels like an eternity until finally, our blissful moment fades, and reality slowly creeps back in. I'm panting, dots peppering my vision. Shifting, I expect the three men to move around me, changing positions like a carousel. Rotating to give each a turn—but that's not what happens. Instead, I'm eased up the mattress, cocooned in by the hard planes of their bodies. They've barely broken a sweat, so the break is for my benefit. I don't question it, not as I instinctually snuggle into Kyan's side, my limbs as heavy as my voice.

"Lucas?" I breathe. "You were never going to give me back my meds, were you?" Of all the times to ask such a question, this is most likely the worst. But I don't want to fall asleep beside them with it playing on my mind. Cupping my cheek, Lucas gently twists my head backward to see the serenity in his gaze.

"No, Feisty One. I was never going to let you dull your true self. From the moment you propositioned Ezra in the library, I wanted you as mine. Not some drugged-up version, but the version of yourself you were scared to let the world see."

Tears well in my eyes, spilling over as I close my lids. Lucas presses a kiss to one side, Kyan kissing away the other. Ezra has settled himself between my legs, his head on my thigh. He's not as open as the others, not as able to express himself, but I understand. In small glimpses, Ezra has shown me he wants affection, but like me, he struggles to accept it. Hiding behind a mask is far easier. Turns out the Thorn Brothers were as desperate for acceptance as I was.

Tiredness drags me into a soft lull, my breathing becoming deep. Yet, there's a smile on my face. I'm officially their pet now. Publicly claimed, fully initiated. The one who will connect them before life tears them apart. We all have our role to play here, and as I lie in a cage of their protection, I vow not to regularly take meds again. I don't want to live on synthetic highs–I want this. Adrenaline rushes and natural thrills. Lucas believes in me, and it's time I believed in myself. The Thorn's Pet is perfect, chosen, revered. It may not be forever, but for now–it's exactly what I need.

"I'm so glad you chose me to be your last one," I murmur, drifting to sleep before I can hear a response.

Several Weeks Later.

Do you believe in déjà vu? How about the pre-emptive feeling something bad is about to happen? That's what I've had since the moment I opened my eyes.

This was my fourth university. My fourth chance to get things right. And I did. Until now. Staring at the ceiling, I feign sleep. Whatever it takes to keep the snoring beings crushing me from either side to stay blissfully unaware of what today is. Graduation day.

The tremors returned in the early hours of this morning. It's been so long since I felt them, I hadn't realized the panic attack was clawing up my throat until it was already in full swing. Somehow, I managed to keep it to myself, finding solace in Ezra's heavy arm as he turned and slammed it down on my ribs. Lucas shifted next, suffocating me into his chest. His cologne lingered, filling my shallow gasps until I could settle enough. This is safe. This is home, I kept repeating.

I didn't get back to sleep, preferring to savor the moments I had left, wrapped in their comfort. Kyan pulled the short straw tonight in whichever way the guys choose who occupies my bed. But being the last we'd spend together, he wriggled beneath the covers sometime before dawn and laid his head on my stomach. If I were in a calmer mood, I could have laughed at wondering whose morning glory would poke him in the eye first.

*We knew this day was going to come,* Jazzie reminds me from the reserves of my mind. She's been much quieter lately, drowned out by the boys laughing and joking whenever they're not fixated on pleasuring me. It's been quite the distraction leading up to my finals, but not one I'd have changed. Wanting them to see me succeed was motivation enough.

A sudden, hard beeping sounds to my left. I jump, dislodging Kyan's head as I scramble to find Ezra's phone beneath his pillow. He's tucked in the space between the mattress and the headboard, his heavy head guarding it like a freaking, snoring minotaur or something. *Turn off, turn off, you stupid fucking thing.* My thumb hits the snooze too late as three pairs of dazed eyes settle on me. Dammit.

"Morning, Feisty One," Lucas kisses my forehead. "Sleep well?" I reserve my grunt. Had it been any other day, I'd have shoved him out of the bed. Instead, I lie here, my limbs clenched and mind whirring.

"Someone had better get *in* me pronto," I grit through my teeth. All three of them jolt into action. Kyan somehow wins, gripping my hips and yanking me down beneath the covers.

"Yes, Ma'am," he chuckles, his mouth descending on mine.

\*\*\*

Smoothing the robes down over my front, the butterflies in my stomach are back. I peer at myself, fighting the tears that are making my eyes appear strained. This is a good day. A happy one, I tell myself. Exhaling a shaky breath, I position the cap upon my pale blue hair. I've curled the ends into loose rings and taken extra time to apply my make-up. The yellow tassel tickles my cheek, so I flick it aside. The photos from today will sit on my desk in the future, and I don't want to cringe every time I look at them.

As ready as I'll ever be, I exit the bedroom and softly pad my white Converse downstairs. Some things never change. At the base of the stairs, the three Thorn Brothers are waiting for me, warm smiles across their faces. Lucas outstretches his hand as if I'm entering a prestigious ball.

"You look incredible," he whispers, pressing a kiss to my cheek. I scoff.

"I'm wearing the baggiest, black robe," I roll my eyes. Kyan winds his arms around me from behind.

"So are we, but somehow you make them look better." I try to twist around, but he holds me tight, keeping my view on the stairs. Ezra steps into my eyeline, a stole in his hands. Waiting for me to straighten, he lowers the material over my shoulders so that the yellow trim hangs down either side of my lapels. The Waversea initials and crest have been stitched into the fabric. His fingers rub the silk, lingering with a sad smile on his face. I catch his blue eyes quickly skate over my shoulder and return, trying to keep the smile in place. He fails.

Spinning, I manage to twist out of Kyan's hold and see a row of suitcases and boxes lined up by the door. My heart stutters.

"What...what's with the bags?" I start to shake again, all of the orgasms from this morning losing their effect. Lucas twists his lips, trying to find the right words.

"We have to leave after the ceremony. There's a celebration event in Dubai tomorrow evening, and our parents thought–"

"You're going today?!" I gasp. "Like leaving the country...already?!" I can't control my tone or my breathing. Kyan looks at the ground.

"Our private jet is being prepped as we speak." The room begins to spin. I knew today was the last, that we'd be preparing to go our separate ways from tomorrow morning. But not today, not right after graduation. Hands grip mine and bring them between our chests.

"Sophia," Ezra states my name without room for arguing. "This was the deal. Fuck, I wish we'd never taken you on now." Tears swim in my eyes, my lips parting on a choked gasp. Ezra's eyes widen. "Fuck, no. That's not what I meant. I mean–" he grapples for words that don't come. Kyan nudges him aside and grips my shoulders.

"What he means is that parting with you is proving harder than we anticipated. We hoped the fun we'd had would be enough. But it doesn't have to be goodbye forever. You can come visit Ezra and I when we've returned home." My chest caves inwards. Lucas keeps quiet, remaining a few steps away. His green eyes cut into me as I try to maintain a coherent thought. He's not coming back. He's going to Dubai, and he's not coming back.

"The...the celebration," I breathe. Lucas looks away, and that's when I know. They aren't leaving for a festival or lavish gala I'd see splashed all over the news. It's his wedding. My eyes slowly trail back to Kyan, grounding myself in his black gaze. "Yes, I'll try to visit," I nod weekly. The lie tastes like ash on my tongue. I can't bear visiting the Thorn's childhood home without Lucas there. He's the light, the jokester.

"Come on," Lucas closes in to drape an arm over my shoulder. There's no sign of his typical smile. "Let's get you graduated." His words echo in the empty room, and a stab of pain pierces my chest. With every step I take toward the door, I grow more aware of the distance between us. Their presence at my back, usually a comfort in my life, now feels like a reminder of what I'm about to leave behind.

The ride in their sports car is filled with silence no one dares to break. My hand clings tightly to the hem of my robe, my knuckles turning white while I stare at the clock on the dashboard. It's unnerving how time seems to rush forward mercilessly, not caring about our sentiments or wishes. I'd give anything for it to stop right now.

Upon reaching the parking lot outside the auditorium, Kyan helps me out of the car. His touch is gentle as if every caress is laced with regret. We head inside as a unit, hands on the small of my back.

The auditorium is alive with excited chatter. Friends and families catching up, congratulating each other. I quickly scan the room and sigh in relief that my mother is nowhere to be seen. That's a drama I don't need today.

The stage is adorned with banners and streamers in the school colors, a backdrop for the podium where graduates will receive their diplomas. My stalling has meant we're just taking our seats when the lighting is dimmed, all except for a spotlight on the stage.

"Psst," someone taps my shoulder. Letty leans forward when I look back, her smile stretched wide. "We did it!" Pulling me in for an awkward hug, she physically vibrates from excitement.

Regardless of my reservations, Letty has been nothing but supportive these past several weeks. Not as much can be said for the other girls, who let their jealousy hinder any kind of friendship we could have had. But not Letty. She's been a constant comfort both in Mrs. Patrick's lectures and out.

Dean O'Sullivan keeps his introduction short before calling for Letty, our valedictorian, to take the stage. The applause is deafening; rambunctious clapping from every seat while Lucas is whistling through his fingers. In the front row, Letty's parents can't resist rushing in for a quick squeeze, her mom already sobbing. I smile warmly.

"Aren't your parents here?" I whisper to Kyan. He scrunches up his nose.

"They've already flown out to Dubai," he murmurs. "There are lots of preparations to make." I nod slowly, refocusing on the stage. Letty is shaking hands with the board of directors, gripping the speech I've helped her memorize in her hands. Kyan's lips remain by my ear. "I am truly sorry it has to end like this. I hope you'll agree it was worth it. To me, at least, it definitely was."

Turning my head, my nose brushes his cheek. Those black eyes I've never been able to resist sinking into appear even darker in the low lighting.

"I could never regret what we've had," I admit softly. My heart squeezes tightly. As if sensing the weight of our conversation, Lucas' hand slips into mine. Interlocking our fingers, he brings them to his lips, pressing a kiss to my knuckles. Wetness dampens my skin, and I almost whimper, refusing to look at him. Rogue tear drops patter my hand until I force it down onto his lap. I can't take it. This feels too much of a goodbye.

"Welcome, friends, families, faculty, and fellow graduates," Letty's voice rings out clearly through the auditorium. "As this year's valedictorian, I stand before you with a profound sense of gratitude and humility. Today, we stand on the precipice of a new chapter in our lives, ready to step into a world where we are the leading characters." Ezra, sitting past Lucas, snorts.

"You can tell she majored in creative writing." I smirk at my lap. That chapter and character malarky was my own input.

The rest of Letty's speech washes over me like a distant echo. My mind is consumed by everything else. Of the trio of brothers who swept in and turned my life into a manageable chaos, one I could handle. They've fixed the broken parts of me, opened a future I otherwise would have struggled to achieve. I can only hope I gave them what they needed from their pet. A sense of togetherness, memories they can hold close when they're separated.

I squeeze Lucas' hand in mine, hoping to convey everything I cannot put into words. His fingers tighten around mine in response, the warmth from his touch both comforting and heart-wrenching. In such a short space of time, I've come to rely on all three of their personalities to keep mine in check. Kyan's calm demeanor, Lucas' bold energy, Ezra's steady mind. My Thorn Brothers in all their glory.

## CHAPTER TWENTY FOUR

As Letty's speech progresses, inviting cheers and applause intermittently from the crowd, I keep my gaze fixed on the stage. Somewhere deep down, a faint twinge of joy surfaces. She's so beautifully confident, standing tall in front of an auditorium full of people, delivering an eloquent speech that we had spent hours perfecting.

"Finally," Letty finishes with a flourish of her hand, "I would ask all graduates to rise." As one, we all stand. The moment feels surreal. There's a pause before names start being called out for us to go on stage. A soft hum of anticipation lingers in the room, occasionally interrupted by bursts of laughter or animated whispers. Fuck, this is happening.

"This was always how it was going to end," Lucas dips his head. I brush my cheek against his stubble like a lioness needing to feel closer to her king. "I'm so glad it was with you." I squeeze Lucas tighter, worried he'll disappear in the excitement of it all. One by one, graduates cross the stage when their names are called. Every face is beaming with a satisfied smile, stopping for the flash of a camera to cement the moment forever.

My throat constricts, a mixture of tears and terror ripping me in two. My pulse is hammering, my chest is flushed. I'm going to pass out. I'm sure of it.

"Sophia Chambers," Dean O'Sullivan calls out. The cheers from the crowd are a muffled roar in my ears as I slowly walk towards the stage. My legs shake, my toes scuffing on every step. This is everything I've worked towards for years, everything I've made of myself against all odds, and I don't want it. Each step towards the outstretched hand is one further from my boys.

*Snap out of it, woman!* Jazzie growls in my head as I stop before Dean O'Sullivan. I peer up at his face, swallowing thickly. *This is still your moment, and now you have your own personal cheerleaders. Embrace it.*

Tightening my jaw, I nod once and grip the hand before me with a little too much force. The Dean matches my strength, handing me the paper rolled and tied with a red bow. As it grazes my free hand, the auditorium erupts. I startle at the hollers and wolf whistles, my personal cheerleaders standing on their chairs above all others.

"Whoop! That's our girl!"

"You deserve this, Sophia!"

"Show the world who they're fucking with!" A stream of laughter floats from me, a smile cracking across my lips just as the camera flashes. The applause grows louder as the boys start to move, a mini procession rushing through the rows to meet me at the bottom of the steps. I launch myself at them, becoming locked in their arms. Kisses pepper my cheeks and forehead, words of encouragement filling my ears.

My smile refuses to fade, the tears streaming from my eyes no longer from the anticipation of a bittersweet goodbye. The Thorn Brothers saved me from myself. They've fixed me, given me the tools to attack life with my head held high. These tears are joyous ones because even though I know I'm walking out of this hall alone, it's with something other people spend their entire lives searching for. Love in my heart.

One Year Later.

"So basically, your standard FMC is down on her luck, loses her job, catches her boyfriend with her boss. So she grabs a bag and leaves, only to find a mysterious invitation later in the bottom of the bag," I rush out in one excited breath, my eyes wide and cheeks flushed. Gripping the bound pages in my hands, I thrust them towards the panel in front of me. "Said invitation leads her to a club where she's locked in overnight on the Wrath floor with a group of MMA fighters. It was everything our department typically looks for, and then some!"

"I can see you enjoyed it," my boss, Frank chuckles. I've been at this publishing house for several months now, finding my niche in the dark romance department.

"Enjoyed it? I devoured it in less than twelve hours!" It's sad, but true. Pretty much since I left work last night with the manuscript tucked beneath my arm, up until I needed to have a triple espresso and stagger back into the office today. And it was worth every second.

"I highly recommend we publish everything this author touches. She has a way of combining angst, lust, multiple love interests, intricate plots and twists into everything she writes. We'd be fools to pass up such an opportunity."

"Your advice and enthusiasm are duly noted, Sophia. Let me talk figures with my team, and I'll let you be the one to put in the call." I cover my mouth, but the squeal escapes anyway. My boss looks up with a light in his eyes, one I used to know rather well. My mind tries to wander but the shadow on the other side of the glass door beckons me to step away for now. Thanking the panel for indulging me forty-five minutes longer than intended, I step out into the hallway, practically vibrating with excitement.

"Well, how did it go?" my best friend asks. Once upon a time, it would have been Jazzie keeping me company, but those days are over. I turn and throw myself into Letty's arms.

"Amazingly! They're going to sign the author to us. You know what that means," I wiggle the manuscript. "I get first look at all of her works from now on!"

"Okay well, as happy as I am for you—it's well past lunchtime, and it's Taco Tuesday. Only a true friend would wait around this long for you to finish blabbing out the entire storyline of the book she's pitching."

"I didn't blab the whooooole story, I didn't say anything about the gut-wrenching, heartbreaking twist where—"

"Yeah, yeah. You can talk at the side of my face while I eat," Letty rolls her eyes. Sliding her arm into mine, she drags me down the hallway and past Becca, who is sitting at my assistant desk, waiting to give me a whole stack of post-it notes to check through. I give her a small smile while Letty forces me into the opulent elevator. This past year has been a whirlwind of hard work and lucky breaks.

After graduation, I was hired on the spot at my first interview, and the following Monday, I was sitting in a booth beside Letty. We've managed to rise through the ranks together, growing closer day by day until we officially became roommates. Our apartment is what I like to call, miniature chic. The abstract painting which Isabella Thorn sent over takes up our entire living room wall. We're rarely home anyway, always working overtime as editorial directors. Although, I don't mind as we can allow ourselves certain freedoms. One including longer lunch breaks and all at the company's expense.

Her stomach is growling as we rush through the main lobby, glass reflecting across the marbled flooring. The sunlight isn't deceiving, as we tumble into the busy street and sigh at the warmth of summer. We fly to Europe next week, touring Italy from Venice to Rome and everywhere in between. I can't wait, and the best part—I don't have to declare all of my medication each time I fly anymore.

The Thorn Brothers did many things to my body, and my mind, but the one I'll always hold dear is boosting my self-worth. I haven't touched an antipsychotic since my Waversea days, swapping my remedy of choice to therapy instead. Along with Dr. Ramsey, we've delved deep into my need to surround myself with imaginary characters. They were a defense mechanism, and like fight-or-flight, the height of my unease triggered them.

Now, I only see Jazzie when I want to. To tell me if an outfit looks good or if I should have another shot. She keeps me on the precariously thin line between good and devilishly naughty. I haven't had any other characters assault me since—not from books at least. Lucas, Ezra and Kyan…they often bleed from my dreams into everyday life, just to remind me how amazing our twelve weeks together were.

"Earth to Sophia, I was talking to you about Italy," Letty snaps her fingers before my eyes. I blink rapidly, realizing we're at the restaurant next door already. A cute, small establishment which is always heaving. Waving to the owner behind the bar, the middle-aged jolly man chastises us for being late.

"Blame it on me," I smile sweetly, navigating the occupied seats to our reserved table in the back. Thanks to the weather, the sliding doors have been pulled back, with only a small fence dividing our seats from the street outside. "Okay, talk to me—I'm ready," I nod, laying a cloth napkin over my lap to protect the expensive pantsuit.

"So, packing," Letty continues, "I was thinking to only take little summer dresses and interchangeable sandals. Easy access for the Italian lovers I'm going to find," she winks. It's my turn to roll my eyes.

"As long as you don't bring them back to the hostel. We're sharing a bunk bed." A basket of breadsticks is placed between us, one automatically finding its way to my hand. Chewing absentmindedly, I start off thinking about how many books on the 'to-be-read' list I'll be able to get through on my eReader whilst away, but soon divert to thinking about this apparent heat wave. I wonder if Lucas will be affected by it too. I wonder a lot of things about Lucas, mainly if he's okay.

I've purposely avoided searching him up online, knowing his wedding would have made the news. Ezra and Kyan too, no doubt, have gone on to take the world by storm. Championship basketball players, dating A-list celebrities, attending all the latest premieres and award ceremonies. Luxurious lives for lavish men, and I'm happy for them. Truly. What we had—all four of us—was incredible, beyond my wildest delusions, and memories I will always treasure.

But life goes on. I meant something to them once, but not anymore. I have no claim to Lucas, and without him—it wouldn't feel right with the others. No, I promised myself not to dwell, only appreciate.

"Oh, for fuck's sake," Letty groans. "Will you stop drooling all over that breadstick? Is my voice really so bland that you zone out every time I speak?" I chuckle, Letty's words reminding me of Mrs. Patrick. I spent the second half of the semester imagining her as a squawking dodo after Ezra rushed me through the coursework with weeks to spare.

"Take it as a compliment, your voice is just too melodic." Sharing a smile, a waitress brings us two mojitos on the house. We shouldn't really drink whilst on our lunch break, but Letty and I are already in full vacation mode. It's only Tuesday, yet we've finished all of our tasks way ahead of schedule. Those which need revising later in the week, we've delegated to interns.

"Do you miss them?" Letty asks, catching me off guard as I sip my drink. I don't need to ask who she means–the three men I *never* speak of out loud. Although I'm certain, she hears me moaning their names in my sleep through the walls of our apartment.

"Of course I do. I know it's stupid–" I sigh.

"It's not stupid at all." Letty's brown gaze holds a rare seriousness. "I saw them with the other Pets. They were different with you." I know this. Even without ever seeing the brothers glance at anyone else, I could feel how in tune they were with me. Like our hearts all beat to the same drum; it was easy, it was natural. We studied together at the dining table, worked out together in the private gym, and made endless love on any available surface. And even when our time was coming close to an end, there was no bitterness. Only understanding.

"Remember how you almost missed your finals?" Letty chuckles, and I groan.

"Oh, don't even. I only made it thanks to Lucas causing a distraction at the door so I could stand on Kyan's shoulders and jump through the window!"

"Where was Ezra?"

"Sporting the black eye I gave him after he finally found the handcuff key and released me from the bedframe," I smirk. I'm sure he did it on purpose, losing faith in his own tutoring. He had nothing to worry about–his constant grillings meant I passed with flying colors.

"Makes for a good story, though," Letty tilts her head and raises her glass.

"I'll drink to that," I agree. Downing my drink, the cocktail glass has yet to touch back to the table when Letty's eyes widen just over my shoulder.

Probably some hot guy on the street has her all flustered, her cheeks turning pink.

"Hey, Feisty One," a deep rumble sounds. I brush my ear with my shoulder, shaking out the imaginary voice. Jeez, what was in that drink? "Long time no see." Letty's mouth is open now, and my brow furrows. Wait–that's not a delusion. Standing in a rush, I spin and come face to face with an overly tanned version of Lucas. A crisp black suit hugs his muscled frame, those biceps appearing to strain against the jacket. His auburn hair is a flash of vibrant red, his green eyes beaming down at me. My mouth turns dry, no words forming.

"Sorry it took so long. I had some...legal affairs I needed to straighten out." My gaze leaves his easy smirk and travels down to the hands clasped in front of him. No wedding ring in sight.

"You," my voice is too breathy, "you didn't get married?"

"It wasn't fair on anyone to lie. My heart belongs elsewhere, and I'm here to claim it back." I don't breathe. Don't dare move in case this perfect scenario shatters and I suddenly wake up. But then, it gets even better.

"We all are." Kyan steps into my eyeline, all shaggy black hair and endless onyx eyes. In direct contrast with his blond curls and icy blues, Ezra appears from Lucas' other side, completing the trio. *My trio.*

"You mean, all of you and me? You all want just me?" I echo back like a parrot. My mind reels to catch up. One semester was the plan. An encapsulated amount of time we all agreed on. But this? Now? My eyes remain on Ezra, his acceptance the one I need to hear the most.

"Get in the fucking car, Sophia," Ezra growls, jerking his head to the Bentley pulled up behind. "We're taking you home." Through his scowl, a small smile breaks free and my heart flutters. I vault over the mini fence without a second thought, diving into their arms. Any and all arms who will have me. Lips touch my forehead before I'm tugged across the sidewalk. I call back for Letty to tell work I've gone home sick for the rest of the day. Probably the week.

"Bitch, don't forget about Italy!" she hollers, waving a breadstick at me. Dropping into the back seat and closing the door, I lean through the open window, but it's Lucas who responds from the driver's seat.

"We've upgraded your trip. A limo will pick you up next week to bring you to the private jet. Hope you don't mind a couple of tagalongs." Kyan, beside me in the back, angles himself across my thighs.

"And about those Italian lovers," he shouts for everyone nearby to hear. "No need to hold back. You've got your own penthouse suite to fill." My mouth drops open as the blackout window starts to rise. Before it reaches the top and shuts me away from the outside world, Letty's whooping slips through.

"Your boyfriends are the best!"

"Yeah, they really fucking are," I agree, catching all three sets of hungry eyes on me. My teeth sink into my bottom lip, the atmosphere tripling with lust, and I already know—this vehicle isn't going anywhere until I'm wrought with pleasure and three orgasms deep.

"*That's my girl*," Jazzie winks from the passenger seat, propping heart-shaped sunglasses over her eyes and waving goodbye as she fades away for the last time.

# Epilogue

Sand squishes between my toes as we walk along the most pristine beach. It's exactly like the brochure. Not a rogue shell or strand of seaweed to be seen along the shore. The sun has just begun its descent towards the horizon, a lazy stroll much like the one Ezra and I are taking. Hand in hand, we reach the lone bar at the far end, replenish our cocktails, and circle back to where our towels are waiting.

"I could spend every day like this," he grins. A smile I'll never tire of seeing, but right, with a golden glow cast across the tilt of his lips, he's flawless. Even with his mess of blond curls speckled with sand. We walk slowly, savoring our solitude until we reach our belongings. Settling back on my towel, I lean on Ezra's broad shoulder and click our glasses together.

"Here's to our last night in Australia," I cheer. Ezra's smile wobbles slightly as he downs the pink liquid in one. It's been three weeks since we parted ways with Letty, who flew directly home from Italy. I fully expected to be returning with her, but the Thorns had other plans. Ones which included a sightseeing trip from Perth to Melbourne and many dives into the Great Barrier Reef. Three blissful weeks, but reality is right around the corner.

"It'll be okay, you know," I reassure Ezra. He's been on edge all day, drinking since around ten o'clock this morning.

"I hope so," Ezra murmurs. He avoids my gaze, tucking his head into my neck to watch the others.

Kyan and Lucas are in the water, their muscular forms cutting through the waves as they surf. Watching them brings a smile to my face; their laughter and energy are infectious. Ezra, on the other hand, won't leave my side, even if he's nervously twiddling his mini umbrella. I sip on my cocktail, stroking my left hand over his thigh.

Needless to say, I've barely had a flicker of anxiety since arriving on the island. Not even the suitcase of skimpy outfits without a long-sleeved top in sight has unnerved me. The boys take the time to kiss my scar every day, reminding me how beautiful they think I am. Their confidence, their pride, their affection. It's all more than enough to remind me I'll never be alone again.

"Hey, Sophia! Watch this!" Kyan calls out, waving frantically from the ocean as he and Lucas ride a rolling wave toward the shore. Lucas starts to wobble, but instead of going down gracefully, he dives at Kyan and takes them both down. I can't help but laugh, their antics continuing as they scuffle and shove each other out of the water.

A gentle breeze carries the salty scent as it ruffles my hair. I watch Kyan and Lucas laughing as they walk towards us, surfboards under their arms, water droplets glistening on their tanned skin. Every muscle in their matching sets of washboard abs winds me into a delicious state of sated and starving.

"Did you have fun?" I ask, unable to keep the smile off my face.

"Always," Lucas grins, settling down next to me on the sand. Kyan takes his place at my feet, using his wet hands to slowly massage them.

"Tell us, Sophia," Kyan raises a brow. "What are your plans when we get back home?" I take a deep breath, feeling the weight of the question. None of us have discussed where exactly home for me will be once we touch back down on American soil.

"I mean...I suppose most of that depends on you guys, really. I love my job at the publishing house, but I have been thinking. The distance has given me some clarity, and I...well, I'd like to search for a charity for people who struggle with anxiety and addiction. See if I can volunteer and help in any way." Ezra reaches out and squeezes my hand.

"They'll be lucky to have you," he ensures, sincerity lacing his words. I swallow, lowering my gaze. Still, after all of this time, it's Ezra's praise I struggle to accept the most.

"Thank you." I smile at my feet, feeling my heart swell with their unwavering support. I decide then to stop leaving things unsaid, to get some answers once and for all. "What about you guys? What do you see for our future?" Yep–ours, because I'm not going anywhere. That's a fact. I lick my dry lips, finishing the rest of my cocktail when the silence stretches on.

Ezra takes my glass, drumming against the side as he stares out at the water. Everyone seems to be watching him, waiting for him. Nerves try to flutter inside my chest, but I tamper them down. It's odd, seeing Ezra so uneasy, but I don't want to push him. We all have our moments of anxiety. Of uncertainty. He hesitates for a moment more, casting a glance at his brothers before turning to me.

"Kyan and I have been planning to set up our own business for a long time now, when we thought Lucas would be..." Ezra's eyes dart back to the sea. "Now we've got to find a role for this knucklehead, cleaning toilets or something." Lucas reaches across to punch his brother in the arm. I roll my eyes and bite down my smile. I'm staying out of it. "But regardless of what happens, we want you to know that we'll always be here to support you. Whatever you want to do, wherever you want to go, count us in."

"We'll always be by your side, Feisty One." Lucas nods in agreement, his green eyes shimmering in the sunset.

"No matter what," Kyan adds, his voice firm and resolute. "We won't be separated again." My eyes start to swim, the fruitiness of the cocktail and salty breeze getting to me. All of their hands are touching me, Ezra's fingers lightly stroking my scar. I've known from the start, from the evening Lucas first propositioned me with his contract, this was different. They didn't treat me like a possession, but rather, they gave me control. They didn't ridicule me for my past, or for my anxiety, but provided the tools for me to overcome them. If that's not love, I don't know what is.

"You guys are everything to me," I whisper, choked up by the intensity of what I feel inside. As if my next breath belongs to each one of them. The heavy thump of my heart, the fibers of my being. I'd surrender it all to keep their eyes fixed on me the way they currently are.

"I'm so fucking glad you said that," Ezra sighs in relief, his voice trembling slightly as he reaches into his shorts pocket and pulls out a small velvet box. "Because there's something we really want to ask you." Shifting to kneel beside me, Ezra opens the box. My entire world stutters to a halt.

Set in gleaming platinum, the three bands interlock around a series of stones which glisten like stars against the sunset. The diamonds, I quickly realize, are distinctly different. A pale blue aquamarine, a vibrant green emerald, and a dazzling stone akin to onyx black. One for each brother, as if their souls have been captured in the single piece of jewelry being presented to me now. I forget how to breathe.

"We're in love with you, Sophia," Lucas breathes my name in a desperate whisper. "We have been for over a year, and not being with you was hell for us all."

"We can't do it again," Ezra adds. I manage to draw my gaze upwards to meet his. The vulnerability I find there shakes me to the core. Not that I believe the others would lie, but with Ezra, I always know I'm getting the truth. If I'm being honest, I've seen the truth written all over his face for weeks now. Ezra loves me. They all do.

"Will you marry us, Sophia?" Kyan asks. "All of us?" His grasp on my ankles has tightened, eliminating the possibility of me running away. But I'm not running. I'm exactly where I'm supposed to be. When my eyes lower to the rings once more, Lucas curls his arms around my middle, his wet torso pressing to my back.

"Please. Say yes." He pleads, creating a physical cage around me. One that doesn't suffocate or panic me, but feels like home. They are my home, the only family I'll ever need.

"Yes," I breathe, feeling the weight of my decision settle over me like a warm embrace. It soothes away every last trace of worry I had left, filling me with so much love, I could burst. A moment passes where I don't think anyone heard me until a round of hollers break out. I'm caught in their crushing embrace just as the sun dips out of view. Strings of twinkling lights come to life, illuminating the rolling waves slowly crashing against the shore. I memorize the scene, the feelings spreading through me. Ezra pulls back first to slip the monstrous ring onto my finger, sealing the promise we've made. He kisses it, then lowers his head onto my lap.

"We don't care how or where. We will make it work." Lucas stays at my back, allowing me to recline against him while Kyan tucks into my side. My hands find their hair, absentmindedly stroking. Later, we'll no doubt party all over the villa they've rented. We'll fuck in every room until morning, cementing the crazed, unconventional love we've found. But for now, soaking in this moment is perfect. It's simple, real, and I couldn't have imagined it better myself.

# Acknowledgements

Thank you so much for reading Sophia's story! This isn't one which was on my radar to write, previously being a mini newsletter freebie, but there was a demand for more. More lust, more character development and more hilarious moments between the four of them. I must also thank you for giving me this opportunity, because I've thoroughly enjoyed bringing a more in-depth story arc to life!

For everyone who begged me for more, I hope I've done you proud.

**A special thanks to:**

**Jo** for her incredible editing skills and constant companionship.

### And of course, my readers.

It's plain and simple; I'm nothing without the readers who support me! Thank you all for devouring my books, and also becoming my friends. I love getting to know you, seeing your gorgeous book shelves and building connections with so many talented and wonderful people.

If you're a new reader to Maddison – welcome to the Mole's Burrow!! Maddison is a married mum of two, and a serial daydreamer. As a huge fan of all romance tropes herself, it was time to pen the stories which consume her mind most hours of the day.

As a child, Maddison was a jet setter and has lived all over the world, only to return to the south east of England, where she is now happily settled. With a double award in applied arts and art history, Maddison is a creative with a dark passion for feisty females and spicy stories.

Join my Newsletter via my website:
www.authormaddisoncole.com

Facebook – **Author Maddison Cole**
www.facebook.com/Maddison.cole.314

Facebook readers group - **Cole's Reading Moles**
www.facebook.com/groups/colesreadingmoles

Instagram and TikTok - **@authormaddisoncole**

If you enjoyed Jazzie's cocky and brash ways, I'd suggest you dive into Candy's world at your earliest convenience! Candy runs circles around the biker gang who unknowingly get in her way, aided by her imaginary gummy bear best friend. This pair will leave you in stitches, while the Gambling Monarchs bring the spice. The series is complete to binge now!

## *Other Works:*
## I Love Candy
### Dark Humor RH - Completed
- Findin' Candy (novella)
- Crushin' Candy
- Smashin' Candy
- Friggin' Candy

## All My Pretty Psychos
### Paranormal RH with ghosts and demons - Completed
- Queen of Crazy
- Kings of Madness
- Hoax: The Untold Story (novella)
- Reign of Chaos

## Bound by Fate
### Fated Mates Shifter Romance
- Moon Bound

## A Deadly Sin
### MMA Fighter BSDM RH - Standalone
- A Night of Pleasure and Wrath

## A Wonderlust Adventure
### A Twisted Menage Retellling
- Descend into Madness

- Embrace the Mayhem

### **The War at Waversea**
#### Basketball College MFM Menage - Completed
- Perfectly Powerless

- Handsomely Heartless

- Beautifully Boundless

### **Co-Writes**
- Life Lessons with Emma Luna

Printed in France by Amazon
Brétigny-sur-Orge, FR

19718691R00117